CONTENTS

COMPANIONS OF SAINT FRANCIS OF ASSISI

Brother Angelo Returns to Assisi

Roderic Petrie, O.F.M.

ST. ANTHONY MESSENGER PRESS

Cincinnati, Ohio

Cover illustration by Chris Sickels
Cover design by Constance Wolfer
Book design by Mary Alfieri
Electronic pagination and format by Sandy L. Digman

ISBN 0-86716-448-4

Published by St. Anthony Messenger Press
www.AmericanCatholic.org
Printed in the U.S.A.

INTRODUCTION

ANGELO OF RIETI, friend and companion of Saint Francis of Assisi, was possibly born the same year, 1181, but died maybe thirty years after his friend, perhaps in 1254. Little is known of his life with certainty, beyond the city and region of his origin, because of the confusion which exists with another Angelo (Tancredi), likewise a companion of Francis and one of his earliest followers. The latter Angelo was a native of Assisi, a nobleman and a very wealthy man, of the locally powerful Tancredi family, and was noted for his kindness and good manners. It is not always clear in the early writings which Angelo is being cited. The other Angelo, from Rieti or that region, was of more common origins and had some talent as a musician and troubadour. He, along with Brothers Rufino and Leo, are thought to be the authors of *The Legend of the Three Companions*. The following narrative is an account of events taken from this work, telling the story of Saint Francis and his friends as they might have been, an account by a Brother Angelo who also might have been.

CHAPTER

᏶1Ꮚ

THE SUMMIT OF MOUNT SUBASIO that May morning was thick with flowers, and bees hummed contentedly as they went about their work. I wondered idly if any of them had come from the brothers' hives at the hermitage, whose caves nestled among the oaks in the thick forest below me.

The climb from Spello, and my accumulated years, had left me winded, forcing me to sit on a rocky shelf while I paused to catch my breath before starting down the mountain to Assisi, which lay down there in the valley, still shrouded in the morning mist. Perhaps I should have taken the longer valley route that skirted the edge of the mountain. But the road over the crest of Mount Subasio, the road I had taken so often with Francis and the others years ago, seemed more appropriate. One memory that I wanted to revisit was here, at this ledge of rock, not of a May morning but one in November, almost forty years ago, when Francis and I sat here together and looked out over the Umbrian Valley hidden from us then, not by a morning mist but by smoke from the fields below, where farmers were burning off the stubble of the autumn harvest. So much that morning was hidden from our view.

For several years I had felt no desire to return here to Assisi. "Why torment myself?" I reasoned. Others had told me of the huge church—a monument—Brother Elias had erected over the tomb where Francis lay, of the money collected to pay the stonemasons who built it, of the changes in the way the friars lived at St. Mary of the Angels. "Better not to go," I told myself.

But the time had come now to return, to remember those years when as a young man I came here to join Francis and the other friars. And remembering, I want to write it down for others, separating as best I can the wheat from the chaff, the truth from fable. Already there is enough chaff, too much fable, people adding fiction to his life. There is no need! His life was fabulous enough without any embroidery. So, while there is still time, for the Lord will surely call me home before long, I want to write down what I remember for those who will come in future years.

My name is Angelo. Angelo of Rieti most people call me, to distinguish me from Angelo Tancredi, my fellow friar and friend who comes from down there in Assisi. He was a knight, the first knight to join Francis and one of his first followers, a wealthy man from a locally powerful family. I, on the other hand, come from good but simple farmers near Rieti. My parents were able to provide me with something of an education, which I have been able to develop on my own. And I early on had a talent for music, an ear for the ballads that wandering minstrels sang at the fairs and on mar-

4

ket day. I, too, when work permitted, used to sing at the regional fairs, joining in the competitions for a prize or just for the applause which I loved to hear. That is how I met Francis.

He and Brother Giles, a young farmworker from near Assisi, perhaps the third man to join him, had come to Rieti to preach. A Saturday late in October it was, a market day, between the grape harvest and the gathering of olives. My father had sent Mariannina, my older sister, and me to barter our excess chestnuts at the market. Neither of us had married, both staying on with our parents. She, I used to tell her, because she was too ugly; and I, she used to retort, because no girl was stupid enough to have me. But she had a head for business, let me tell you, letting no one get the better of her in a trade. So I left her to do the haggling while I took my lute and went off to see if I could find an appreciative audience. I have to admit that people liked my ballads, and I would often get a few coins in my hat to make it worth my while.

Although the sun was bright, the air coming down from the Apennines at that time of year had an autumn crispness in it that animated everyone so that voices seemed louder, gestures more forceful, the square more alive than usual. Heading toward the fountain across the piazza from the cathedral I noticed a sizable crowd there listening to a monk or some sort of preacher. Actually there were two, both dressed in patched and frayed tunics of the cheapest cloth, more like sackcloth, with ropes tied around themselves as belts. Both looked in need of a decent meal. One, whom I later discovered was Francis, was standing on the top step of the fountain, preaching to the people in a rather pleasant but clear voice. The other one kept pointing to him, nodding his head, and shouting: "He's right! Listen to him. He knows what he's saying."

What did he say? I can't fully remember. I know that I stood still in the piazza, maybe forty feet away, clutching my lute in front of me. He was talking about the sin of ingratitude, I know, saying that God had blessed us with many lovely gifts in the world around us yet we never take the time to thank God for such marvelous things as the sun that warms us, the water that quenches our thirst, and so on. But I was mesmerized by the man himself. He was evidently thoroughly convinced of what he was saying, so caught up into his sermon that he was fairly dancing on the stone step. His gestures, pointing to the sun, which he called our brother, were generous. His body was in constant motion and his feet moved, as I say, as though he was dancing to some tune that only he could hear. Maybe that is what caught my attention; he was singing a song, a divine melody, that I could almost, but not quite, hear within myself. It was then that I knew that this man had a melody, a song of divine mystery and pure love that I had to hear. I knew all of the *chansons de Roland*, the epic ballads of *King Arthur and the Round Table* and more, but none of those could feed an enthusiasm or inspire such fervor as filled this little preacher. What was the fire that I could sense burning within him? I wanted to know.

When he had done and was making his way toward the cathedral door, I intercepted him. Francis Bernardone he said his name was, from Assisi, and his companion, Giles. He, too, was from Assisi, he said, but from one of the farms in the valley near Spello. Several years ago I had spent a few days in Assisi, during the May celebrations. It was a fairly large town, but that is all it still is, not to be compared to Perugia, its rival and antagonist, twenty-some kilometers to the north. Of course it did have an impressive fortress at the upper part of the town, but I had heard that the people stormed it a few years back while the duke was away, and declared themselves a commune. Energetic and hardworking, was my impression of them, people who loved their Valley of Umbria. And well they should, for it was a fertile area producing much wheat, and on the mountain slopes the olive trees gave some of the best oil I've tasted.

Francis told me that he intended to stay on for the feast of All Saints on Wednesday and would be preaching there in the square every day. I determined that I would be there to hear him, for he intrigued me. There was something about him that I couldn't put my finger on, that was attractive. He seemed so earnest, so genuine. As I said, his sermon had not really caught my attention; that is, he did not surpass our own parish priest in what he had to say, but the way he said it certainly was different. He was convincing, and his enthusiasm stirred me beyond what a more learned preacher

7

might have been able to do. Anyhow, I wanted to hear him, and watch him, again.

Later that afternoon, when I was singing some French ballads a *jongleur* from Provence had taught me, I noticed Francis and Leo join the circle of people who had gathered around. To my surprise, Francis joined in with some of the songs, and at the end he clapped the loudest of anyone. But no coins from him went into my hat, not that I expected anything from that ragged pair.

"How do you know those songs?" I asked.

"From my mother," he replied with a smile. "She comes from Provence, and I've been there with my father when he went to buy cloth for the business. He's a cloth merchant. Mother used to sing those songs when I was young and she was feeling homesick. You bring back memories of home," he said, a bit wistfully, I thought.

"You say your *father* is a merchant? What about you? Aren't you your father's son? My dad is a farmer. I'm a farmer. My family is a family of farmers."

"That's not for me," Francis grunted. "I tried it, but I was not cut out to be a cloth merchant. If I'm to sell something, I want to sell *God*! Actually, I'm *giving* him away. Like you, I'm a jongleur, a troubadour for the Lord. I, Giles here, and some other brothers like us, are heralds of the King of kings. We're selling real estate: the Kingdom of Heaven. Would you like to reserve a mansion for yourself?"

"It looks to me like your job isn't paying very well," I retorted, looking at their coarse and patched tunics, their bare feet. "You look like you could use something to eat, and I'll bet you don't have any place to stay here in Rieti, do you?"

At the mention of something to eat Giles seemed to take a more keen interest in the conversation. He glanced at Francis, wondering, I guess, if there would be a place for them to stay and maybe something to eat.

"Jesus didn't have a place to lay his head sometimes," Francis tossed back at me, "so it would be an honor for us to follow his example. We're not worried. The Lord supplies those things as needed."

Giles pointed to Francis with his thumb and nodded in complete agreement.

"Do you mean you really don't have any place to stay tonight? You can't sleep out in the open. It's not summer anymore, you know! It's too cold for that now. And the night watchman won't take kindly to two tramps sleeping in the cathedral porch, either, if that's what you have in mind. Look, you had better come home with me. We have plenty of room and my parents won't mind a bit."

"There," Francis laughed, "what did I tell you, Giles? Do you see how God provides for those who trust in him?"

Giles pointed at Francis with his thumb and nodded his head at me, smiling.

I had to laugh, too, at these fellows' good humor. "Well," I said, "come on. We might as well get started before it gets any later. First we have to gather up my sister Mariannina in the market behind the cathedral, and then we'll be on our way."

As we started down the alley between the cathedral and the bishop's residence, we ran right into Mariannina.

"I was just coming to look for you," she hollered. She always speaks loudly because she is a little deaf. "Look at all the flax I got in the trade. What a wonderful time I had! I and that woman from Ostia really went at it, but I got the better of her. Now how am I going to get it home?" It was true, she was loaded down with bundles of flax, and dragging some bundles along behind her.

"Brother Giles and I will give you a hand," suggested Francis, reaching out to relieve her of a big bundle of flax.

"What?" she yelled at him, keeping the flax out of his grasp. "Who are these ragamuffins, Angelo?" she asked me, eyeing Francis and Giles suspiciously. "Are these some more of your vagabond friends looking for a handout? If they think they can sing me a song and get a handful of money, they've picked the wrong woman!"

Francis laughed and shouted at her: "No, Miss Mariannina, we're not minstrels, and we don't want your money. But we would like to help you with your bundles."

Mariannina visibly relaxed her grip on the flax, so Francis and Giles both lifted a bundle on their shoulders and off we went, Mariannina leading the way out the east gate and up the road toward home.

Later that evening we all sat around the table after our meal of sausages and bread. I noticed that both Francis and Giles, although loud in their praises for the bread Mother had freshly baked and my father's pork sausages, with lots of garlic and hot pepper, ate very little and drank only a bit of wine. The night air had become chill so the fire in the hearth felt good as we watched the tongues of flame hungrily lick the oak logs. Now and then sparks would jump up the chimney as the wood crackled with the heat. An ember fell from the hearth and lay near Francis' foot, where it quickly died.

"Like a soul separated from God," he said. Somewhere near the hearth a cricket chirped. "Listen," Francis said softly, "Brother Cricket is tuning his violin to give us a song."

"What?" said Mariannina. "My brother brought his viola along?"

"No, Miss Mariannina," he said patiently and more loudly. "Brother Cricket is chirping. Can't you hear him?"

"I haven't heard a cricket for years. Nor a bird. It's hard enough to hear people when they shout at me, let alone a cricket. How could I hear a cricket?"

"Would you like to?" he asked. "Would you like to hear the song of the larks, the wind in the trees, the ringing of the church bells down in the valley?"

"Don't be foolish," she said quietly, almost to herself. "Of course I would." She studied her rough, work-worn hands on the table before her. "If I had been able to hear better I would have become a nun long ago. But the nuns would not accept me. It's a cross for me to bear, they told me, that I can't hear, and that God wants me to stay here at home. Well, I've accepted that, but even so, I wish that I could hear that cricket you're talking about. I know that I am needed at home, but if only I could be a nun! Right here! There must be a way that I can give myself to prayer and do some good."

"Oh, there is, Mariannina, and we'll find the way."

"You say you'll pray? Oh, do. Ask God to give me back my hearing and I promise I will never complain about anything again!" And she laughed, seeing the doubt on our parents' faces, and off she went to bed.

We sat there in silence for a few moments, enjoying the quiet and the warmth of the fire. In its glow I looked at Brother Francis' face. His lips moved a bit, so I wondered if I was losing my hearing too, if I had not heard what he said.

"Did you say something, Brother Francis?" I asked.

"No, Angelo. At least not to you. I was asking God to give your sister her wish: to give back her hearing. She would be pleased, wouldn't she?"

I nodded, impressed that Francis took to heart Mariannina's request for prayer.

The next morning I was awakened by distant thunder and the swallows under the eaves announcing a coming storm. Going into the kitchen, there was Mariannina already up, kneeling by the hearth, coaxing, I thought, last night's fire to life.

"What are you doing up so early?" I spoke loudly to her for her back was to me.

"You don't have to shout, Angelo," she said, turning toward me, a strange look on her face. "I can hear you. The cooing of the doves in the cote woke me up. I haven't heard the doves in years! I can hear, Angelo! Just now I was kneeling here listening to that cricket that Brother Francis said was chirping for us last night. I can't find him, but I can hear him!" She stood up and shouted: "I can hear! It's a miracle!"

Mother and Father came running into the kitchen. "What's the matter?" Mother asked. "Is someone hurt? Is there a fire?"

"Mama," Mariannina stammered, "I've been cured! During the night. I woke up and I can hear! Isn't it wonderful? Oh, excuse me for talking so loudly. Where are those two monks or whatever they are? When I asked them to pray for me I had no idea that anything would come of it! They haven't gone have they?"

"We haven't gone yet, Miss Mariannina." It was Francis, and behind him Giles, standing in the doorway. Evidently they had been up before any of us and had been outside. "But we will have to say goodbye soon and get back to town. Giles and I want to be there to preach to the people in the plaza between Masses. Will you be singing ballads there at the fountain, Angelo?"

I shook my head, glancing at my father. He never allowed any singing or music on Sunday. Too frivolous, he said. And he confirmed it:

"No, Sir Brother Francis" (everyone was "Sir" or "Madam" to my father), "Angelo won't be singing his ballads today, but we will be there for the High Mass at the cathedral at ten o'clock. We will look for you. But you are not leaving us, are you? Didn't Angelo tell me that you will be in Rieti until All Saints Day on Wednesday? Please stay here with us. As you see, we have plenty of room now that most of the children have left home."

My mother and I nodded in agreement. And Mariannina grabbed him by the arm. "Oh, Brother Francis, Brother Giles, you must stay here. We won't take a 'no' for an answer. I'll make you some chestnut pudding to thank you somehow for your prayers for me. I'm sure that it was your prayers that God answered, because he has certainly had plenty of my own up to this time and never gave me back my hearing. You two are saints, I know it!"

"Miss Mariannina, Brother Giles and I will take delight in your pudding, I know, and we will be blessed to stay here a few days more, but give your thanks to God for your hearing. I'm sure that he has something special in mind for you and wants you to be in perfect health." It was years later that I learned that Francis despised chestnut pudding, but I recall that he heroically ate every bit that Mariannina put in front of him.

Needless to say, I kept my eye on Francis Bernardone. It was evident to me that something out of the ordinary was going on. He was not one of the run-of-the-mill zealots who would show up from time to time, preach, stir up a few people and then disappear. Many of them were patently crazy. No, this man was different. There was an integrity to him that was captivating, a simplicity that was deceptive, for he was far from being a simpleton. He was prayerful and abstemious, and he seemed to be very intimate with God. So during the next few days I was there whenever he preached in the square. Again, his words were not brilliant nor was his message new. It seemed to me that he was the message. It was evident that he believed what he said, that he had experienced God's love and forgiveness when he told people to rely on them, and that he lived up to what he preached to others.

Wednesday came. The Feast of All Saints. The whole family, the four of us, went to Mass at the cathedral. It was beautiful: The bishop gave a good sermon, the choir outdid itself and we all received Communion. And afterwards we stood with some others listening to Francis preach. It was then that I decided (or God let me know that he had decided) that I was going to ask if I could join him and Giles and the others. What moved me was what he said about the Communion of Saints: that Mary, Peter and Matthew and the other apostles, the holy martyrs, all the saints, were our older brothers and sisters, that we were a family, of the same household. I come from a large family. We were eleven children. So I knew well what it meant to have many family members. I had never thought of the Blessed Virgin as being my older sister. I had never conceived of Saint Joseph or John the Baptizer as being my older brothers, that they were concerned about helping me. I wanted to be a part of the brotherhood that Francis and Giles shared and maybe, if they would let me, tell others that we all have a common Father who loves us.

So that is how it happened that I sat here on this rock, that November morning, alongside Francis, looking down into the new day coming into the Umbrian Valley. I had asked them, Francis and Giles, if I could join them and they welcomed me.

"When can I come to Assisi to join you?" I asked.

"Tomorrow morning you'll return with us," Francis said.

My heart skipped a beat. So soon? How would I prepare my father and mother? How say goodbye to my brothers and sisters, my whole family? But it worked out fine. Mariannina, God bless her, made it easy. When I confided in her, on the way back to the farm, what I had just decided to do and what Francis had said, she insisted that I should go in the morning.

"It's the thing to do, Angelo," she assured me. "Don't you see? God planned all of this. He sent Francis here so that you would receive the call to serve as a brother. He sent Francis here to heal me of my deafness so that I will be able to care for Mama and Papa, and manage the farm, so that I can be the nun I always wanted to be, but right at home. Don't worry about Mama and Papa; they will be fine. And if we need anything, God has blessed us with the family of the saints, as Brother Francis was saying, and our own family."

That night, when I broke the news to my parents, they surprised me. At first Mother cried a bit, but before long they were both smiling and my father

16

insisted on bringing up from the cellar some of the wine he saved for special occasions. He told me to get my lute, even if it was a holy day; he got his old violin and we sang some of our favorite songs. That was my last night at home. Now I have a new home down there in the valley. A new family, new brothers, I have yet to meet.

We started off from Rieti—Francis, Giles and I—to Spello. Giles continued on to visit his parents, not much farther in the valley, but Francis and I stayed the night with some friends of his in Spello, planning to join Giles the next day at St. Mary of the Angels in the woods below Assisi. Then, once again starting early in the morning, we followed a winding trail up the flank of Mount Subasio, across the meadow already touched by autumn frost and paused here on this rock to catch our breath before starting down the path to Assisi.

It's close to forty years ago that I sat here with Francis that November morning. It's cold, as it was that morning. The chill wind from the mountain stirs the mist, hanging like torn rags in the trees, as the sun begins to warm the fields in the valley below. Off to my right and far below me some white doves rise above the trees, circle and disappear into the trees again, frightened by a hawk. That must be the Carceri, the hermitage, where we paused for a drink from the spring on our way down the mountain that day.

It was a place of caves. For hundreds of years hermits had used them, and I suppose bandits and hunters as well. Francis told me that several centuries ago, when monks had fled from the Eastern Empire because of opposition to their use of icons and other holy pictures, many had come to this part of the world, had built little monastic refuges here and there. Most recently monks of Saint Benedict from the Abbey of San Benedetto, about three kilometers farther south along the flank of the mountain, used the caves during the summer as places of prayer. But now a few friars live there, at least in decent weather, and are building a small friary there. Bernardo, Sylvester, Rufino live in some of the caves much of the year. But all of us, those of us from the early days, all of us lived in the forest caves there during the summer months. What a blessed place!

Francis, even before he left the world to lead a life of penance, used to go up to those caves, drawn by the Holy Spirit, to be instructed in what he should do with his life. In the face of the cliff, below the little chapel built by the early monks in one of the caves, was another grotto that faced out on the gorge that widened to the Umbrian Valley. That was where Francis loved to go. He would spend hours there in prayer, sometimes days. It was there, he told me, that he had learned peace.

I know that is true. I always loved to go there to the caves. The night would be so still. Occasionally I would see a star fall across the night sky and silently plummet from sight below the horizon. There was not a sound except for the rustle now and then of a mouse in the dry leaves or the call of an owl off in the woods. It was in that quiet that I learned the stages of prayer. I talked and God listened. God talked and I listened. Neither talked, we both listened. Silence. Peace.

Perhaps the bird's song, the wind's sigh, the brook's incessant murmur are better prayers to our Creator than our own. Who can say? There are times when we become so focused on our own prayer that we find the prayer being offered up by nature around us a distraction. Even Francis discovered that to be true in the quiet of the Carceri. On one occasion when he had gone to his cave to pray for several days, a storm broke on the heights above sending with a fierce roar torrents of water down the chasm below his cave. The constant rush of the water was such a distraction to him that he begged God to divert the water elsewhere. And God did! To this day not a drop of water flows down the rocks below the cave.

On another occasion, Francis became aware of a flock of birds in an oak across the chasm from the cave. They were making an incessant racket, making it impossible for him to keep his mind on his prayer. So he went to the mouth of the cave and scolded them, as one would idle children. "Brothers and sisters," he cried out to them, "it is such a lovely day and here you are wasting your time. Go, as God would have you do, and bring the Good News of his love to the four corners of the world!" He gave them a blessing and didn't they fly off in the four directions of the compass? With a smile he went back into the cave to pray in peace.

The tinkling of the chapel bell from the hermitage

below called to mind the same sound that reached Francis and me as we sat here years ago. "I think that is the bell at San Benedetto calling the monks to prayer, Angelo. We don't have a psalm book, but we could pray with them by saying the Our Father together. Shall we?" And we did. That was the first time I prayed with Francis. Even though it was a prayer we knew by heart, I could sense that he meant every word of it.

"Do you think the Kingdom of God is coming soon, Brother Francis? Is that why you and the others have given up your property and are living poorly? Are you getting ready?" I asked.

"Is the Kingdom coming?" Francis answered. "Angelo, the Kingdom of God is here now. This is it," and he swept his hands out over the scene in front of us.

"Assisi? Umbria? This is the Kingdom of God?"

"Well," he smiled, "in a way, yes. I like to think that this valley is so blessed; but the world, Angelo, the whole world is the Kingdom of God. At least it should be. The birds that fly in the sky, the fish that swim in the waters, the foxes in the woods, they all know it, I'm sure. It's just us, people, who don't know it or don't accept it. That's why it's important for someone to tell people, to remind them, if they have forgotten, that the Kingdom of God is already here. And the Lord Pope himself asked me to do that, to tell people to be good citizens of that Kingdom and subjects of the Lord Jesus and to have nothing to do with the kingdom of this world and the Prince of Darkness."

"So, yes, you're right. I think of Umbria as the

Kingdom of God. Part of his Kingdom, anyway. This is where we live. It's only lately that we have gone anywhere else to preach: to Florence, and Rieti and so on. Only since last year when the pope gave us his blessing.

"We brothers are the poorest and most unworthy citizens in this part of God's Kingdom, Angelo, but God has blessed us. You can't see it, but under the haze down there is a place of peace. I didn't realize that until rather recently, just a few years ago I discovered it, but God has left his footprint down there in the soil of Umbria. He has carved his name on every tree. He has left a fingerprint on every leaf and the smell of him in every flower. It is a blessed place.

"Oh, I know, every valley is the same. That's true. But we don't live in every valley. It's here that I first sensed God's presence in his handiwork, creation, so it's here that I find the Kingdom best. Every plant, every worm and beetle tell me something about God. Like you and me, they are creatures, the imaginings of God. Granted, we have an intellect and Jesus became a man, like us, not a sparrow or lamb. But nonetheless we are all related, as creatures, and often they, the lark and the ox, give praise to our Creator more readily than we. In their own way they point out the Creator to me. Our lesser brothers and sisters help our minds to climb up the ladder of creation to arrive at the top, to the One who made us all. That's why, Angelo, I wanted you to look down this morning on where we're going. Down there I hope you will find out who you are and how you fit into God's tapestry of creation. Now come, let's go down there to see what the Lord has prepared for us."

I picked up my lute that Francis agreed I should bring with me and followed him down the path to the future.

CHAPTER

2

"THE CARCERI HAS CHANGED, Sylvester," I said, leaning back against the wall of the chapel. He and I sat on a bench outside in the morning sun filtering down upon us through the leaves of an old oak tree. The sun's warmth felt good.

"Changed? Yes, I suppose it has. How many years has it been since you were last here, Angelo? Twenty years?"

"Twenty years at least," I agreed.

"Everything changes, Angelo. That's life. Only God remains constant. Even our ideas about God change, but he doesn't. Life goes on with us or without us, and we have to go with it. Or die."

"I know, Sylvester," I sighed. "Tell me, what are the changes here?"

"I remember the day you came down the path with Francis. November, wasn't it? You had just come over the mountain from Rieti where the two of you had met. We were still living in the caves down below the garden, although winter was coming on fast. Now we have this building," and he indicated with his thumb the wall next to us. "As you can see, we just closed up the cave that was there, enlarged it some, too, so now we have a kitchen and dining room in one half and a dormitory in the other. Then we put a wall at the mouth of the cave the old monks used to use as a chapel and there you have it: our church. You remember how cold it gets up here once November comes. We couldn't live up here in the caves during the winter, but now we can. At night we sleep in the dormitory, but usually during the day it warms enough for us to be in our caves or working outside. This has been a hard winter, Angelo," and he held up his hands for me to see. They were swollen, twisted from arthritis, and still bore scabs from chilblains. "I think that when autumn comes I will have to go down to St. Mary of the Angels. It's warmer there. I don't want to be a burden to anyone, though."

"Who else is here, Sylvester?"

"Bernardo, of course. Juniper. Rufino more often than not. Others, sometimes. It depends on the time of year. But always me. Always Bernardo."

"Where is he?"

"Down there in the trees below the garden. The same place he has been all these years. Go see him, Angelo. He will be glad to see you. Go alone. I'm too sore in the knees to go with you. I'm worried about him. He hasn't been well lately."

So I went down the path through the trees to where I knew I would find Bernardo di Quintevalle. The leaves, still wet from a rain during the night, were slippery underfoot. The feel of the cool air on my face, the smell of the wet leaves, brought me back to that time forty years ago when I first met this gentle and genteel man from Assisi.

On a bench made from a split tree trunk, Bernardo sat hunched in a tattered gray mantle. His cropped hair was white now and his square face more gaunt than I recalled. His eyes, however, black, shone like candles in a battered lantern.

"Angelo?" he asked, as I approached him.

"Yes, Bernardo, it's I."

He rose with some difficulty from the bench and we embraced. Through the thin material of the tattered mantle I could feel the thinness of his shoulders.

"Yes," he said, sensing my thoughts. "There's not much left of me. Skin and bones, as they say. More bones than skin, I guess. It's so good to see you again. What brings you back here, Angelo, after all these years?"

"A search, Bernardo. For memories."

"Memories? You're looking for memories?" His eyes looked off into the woods around us where perhaps some memories lurked among the trees. "Come, sit down. I can't stand for very long. We have plenty of them. But you were here in the beginning, Angelo. You remember. You have memories of your own."

"Not in the very beginning, Bernardo. And the memories that I do have need to come back to where they were born."

Whenever Bernardo mentioned the early days of the Order he spoke of "the beginning," as though he was quoting from the Book of Genesis. His eyes came back to me and he smiled, teasing me. "What do you want me to remember for you? It had better be something from years ago because I can't remember what I ate for breakfast, recent things, anymore. You know how it is." He nudged me with his elbow.

"I have the same problem, Bernardo. But yes, years ago; in the beginning, before I met you here that November morning when I came over the mountain with Francis from Rieti. How did you first know Francis? Were you friends as children?"

"I always knew Francis, Angelo. I was a year or two older than him, and as a boy my family lived in the upper part of Assisi, not far from San Rufino, the cathedral. Being a bit older, and living where I did, I had friends that did not include him. But later, in our teenage years, when we would go to parties and jousts, I got to know him. He was an entertainer, Francis was, and he made any party a success. You know how he was."

I nodded. "But weren't you a close friend, a companion?"

"No, not really. I knew him, as I said; I liked him, everyone did, but only later I can say I knew him. When I came of age I inherited some property, some farms, that my grandfather had left me. My father thought it best that I set up my own household, so I moved into a house that the family owned behind the city hall, you know the one, not far from Francis' home.

"Being young, I soon became restless. Being a landlord didn't demand much time or talent, and I was never much for parties or idleness, so I answered the

Holy Father's call to free the holy places. I joined a crusade. The less said about that the better. Anyhow, I served almost three years in the Holy Land. When I returned to Assisi my old friends had a party for me. It wasn't a lively party, no songs, no dancing, and it dawned on me that Francis was not there. When I asked someone where he was, the answer was evasive: that Francis had changed, that he didn't go to parties anymore, that he was no longer fun to be with. I didn't pursue it, but I made up my mind that I would look him up.

"The next morning I asked Concetta—she was the baker's oldest daughter; she used to cook and clean house for me—if she knew anything about Francis Bernardone, the milliner's son.

"Concetta rolled her eyes and said: 'I think he's soft in the head, sir.'

"'What do you mean? What happened to him?'

"'Well, sir, you were gone from here when we had the war with Perugia. It was a terrible thing, and as usual it was us poor people who got hurt the most. But Francis Bernardone did get captured and thrown into prison over in Perugia. He was there a year until his father got him out. It must have cost him a good sum of money, too. I remember when he came home—he was too sick to walk. Some neighbors had to lift him out of the cart they brought him home in and carry him into the house. I don't know whether it was the year in jail or the sickness afterwards, but he became soft in the head.'

"'He's crazy?'

"'I wouldn't say he's crazy, sir. He's not like Pazzo, the town idiot, but he's different from what he was. For several months nobody saw him. He was sick in bed, we heard. Then we would see him sitting in the sun outside his door, thin and pale as milk. He was very pleasant if we stopped to talk to him, but later, when he got some strength back, we didn't hear him out in the streets at night singing with his friends as he did before. We would see him going in or coming out of San Nicolo Church, even during the week.'

"'That doesn't mean there's something strange about him, Concetta. Lots of people go to church to pray.'

"'I know, sir, but he started praying more than most. And he acted different. Do you remember Giorgio Fortini from Rivotorto?'

"I nodded. 'Vaguely. The family has a big farm down there?'

"'That's the one. Giorgio is the oldest. He and Francis have been friends for a long time. The Bernardones own the farm next to the Fortinis. Giorgio has gone off and become a monk up at San Benedetto, but before he went off he and Francis used to go up to the place where all the caves are, the Carceri I think it's called, and they would spend hours, all day, in the caves. Praying! Now don't you think that's strange?'

"'It's certainly not the Francis I knew, but also you said he wasn't feeling well. Maybe it was part of his recovery to go off and be by himself.'

"'Sir, you haven't heard the strangest part yet. Francis started working for his father in the shop again. Things seemed to be going well, so Signore Bernardone went off on a buying trip to Sienna, leaving Francis in charge for a few days. I don't think the poor man was any sooner out of the city gate when Francis loaded up a horse with some bolts of cloth, went off to Foligno and sold everything: cloth, horse and saddle! And he disappeared. His father is back now. Francis' mother, Lady Pica, is worried sick about him, and so is his father, but I think he is more furious than worried. That was a good bit of money Francis cost him.'

"'So Francis ran away? He's gone?'

"'I don't think he has gone far. My brother Flavio was coming home from the mill on Monday, passed by San Damiano, that old church down the hill, and swears he saw Francis down there. He must be hiding from his father. Now isn't that strange? He must be soft in the head.'

"So, Angelo, I rode down to San Damiano. Francis was there, all right. He was sweeping out the church. Never a large person, he was even more thin than I remembered.

"'Hello, Bernardo,' he said, and that was all. He just kept on sweeping. No 'How are you?' or 'Welcome home.' I stood watching him for a moment, and he said: 'Would you bring that shovel over here, Bernardo? You can throw this dirt outside.' So I put my cloak on a chair and I did as he asked. When I came back he was standing looking up at the large crucifix that hangs from a

29

beam over the altar there. You've seen it. I stood next to him and looked up at it, too.

"'It spoke to me, Bernardo,' he said.

"'Spoke to you?' I couldn't think of anything else to say.

"'Yes. Jesus spoke to me. From the cross there. There was no mistaking it. Last month it was. I had run in here to escape a rainstorm. He called me by name: "Francis," he whispered to me, "as you see, my church is falling into ruin. Rebuild my church." That was all. And as you see, Bernardo, it is in a bad way, with a hole in the roof and plaster falling down.'

"'How are you going to go about rebuilding it?'

"'I have some money, enough to pay for it, I think. From a business transaction.'

"'Yes, I heard,' I said. 'In Foligno.'

"'Oh, were you talking to my father? Is he upset?'

"'I don't think "upset" does justice to him. But he's worried about you, too. And so is your mother.'

"'The priest here wouldn't touch the money when I offered it to him. It's up there on the window ledge where I tossed it,' and he indicated the window in the far wall. 'I don't know what to do now. I can't pretend the crucifix didn't speak to me, because it did. Bernardo, I don't suppose you would have the money to…' I shook my head. 'Then I'll have to do it myself. Somehow.'

"But it didn't work out the way he planned. That afternoon a clerk from the municipal court showed up at San Damiano and arrested him. His father had dis-

30

covered his hiding place and now demanded justice for the cloth and the horse Francis had taken and sold. However, when Francis appeared before the judge, he claimed exemption from civil law, saying he had put himself in the service of the Church, and therefore he should be tried by a Church court.

"'Very well then,' said the judge. 'I'll set up an appointment with the bishop for tomorrow morning at nine o'clock. You'd better be there, young man!'

"Concetta told me the next morning the latest news. 'At nine o'clock this morning Francis Bernardone is supposed to be at the bishop's residence for a trial. I bet half the town will be there to see what comes of this!'

"Well, Angelo, half the town was not there, that overcast Tuesday, but there were perhaps thirty to forty onlookers. I was one of them. Francis' father was there, of course, looking grim, along with Angelo, his other son. Lady Pica, too, Francis' mother. She was clearly distressed and her eyes were red from crying. Francis arrived and he, too, looked subdued, but he did not appear nervous. When he looked over toward his father and received no acknowledgment, he turned his attention to the bishop who, wearing a cope and a miter, staff in hand, came out of the door of his residence and into the courtyard.

"A young assistant at his side shouted out: 'Attention, attention! The bishop's court is now in session. Those looking for justice under the law of the Church come forward.'

"Both Francis and his father went and stood in front

of the Bishop. 'Pietro, Francis,' he said, 'what are you doing here? What's the matter? Did the canons at San Rufino neglect to pay their bill again?'

"'Your Grace,' Pietro Bernardone blurted out, motioning toward Francis at his side, 'he took many bolts of cloth from the store, a horse, and without my permission he sold them. He waited until I went away and then he stole from me. He had no right to do that. He has gone too far! I want the money he owes!'

"'Pietro, why come to me with this? This is a matter for the civil court, or for you to settle by yourselves.'

"'No, your grace,' Francis spoke up, 'we were there yesterday, but I claimed exemption. Your grace, I have given my life over to service to the Church.'

"'Yes, well, you're right, then. That's a different matter. Now, then, Francis, is it true what your father is accusing you of? Did you take your father's goods without permission and sell them? Tell the truth!'

"Francis looked embarrassed, but he held his head up and looked at the bishop. 'Yes, your lordship, I admit it. I did. Truthfully, I don't know what possessed me. It was wrong. I knew that I couldn't stay at home any longer, could not be a businessman like my father here, or a soldier, either. Maybe I thought of the cloth and the horse as my inheritance, I don't know.'

"'You must restore to your father what you wrongfully took from him, my son,' the bishop said. 'Do you still have the cloth, the horse?'

"Francis shook his head. 'No, I don't. I sold them in Foligno. It was for a good purpose. To rebuild San

Damiano Church. I got a good price,' and he smiled a bit. Then from his belt he pulled out a leather wallet and held it out to the bishop, who held up a hand to him.

"'Not to me, Francis. Give it to your father.'

"Turning to his father, he handed the wallet to him. 'You're right. This is yours, Father. I'm sorry.'

"Francis' father snatched the wallet. 'That's the truth,' he growled. And turning to the bishop, he said: 'Your grace, this young man is my son, but he has been a great disappointment to me. I have raised him, given him the best I could, put food in his stomach and clothes on his back, and what have I got to show for it? I'm ashamed to admit that I fathered him.'

"Francis, who had been standing there, suddenly stepped away from his father and, turning to all of us forming a semicircle around them there in the courtyard, he said: 'Up till now I have called Pietro Bernardone my father. But from now on I will say only "My father, who art in heaven."' And with that he suddenly stripped himself of his shirt, pants and shoes, and naked as the day he was born he put the bundle at his astonished father's feet. 'There,' he said, 'are the clothes you put on my back.'

"We were all stunned, but the bishop reacted quickly. He threw his cope around Francis to cover his nakedness. But Francis pushed away the brocaded covering and walked out of the town gate, not looking back, as the sun broke through the mist, washing us all in its warmth.

"That was the last time I saw Francis, Angelo, for over six months. Later I heard that a friend of his had given him a tunic to wear but that he would accept nothing else. A story drifted down from San Benedetto Abbey, brought by one of the monks on market day, that Francis had stayed with them for two days as a kitchen helper, but had then left. Much later I learned, from Francis himself, that he had continued on over the mountain to Gubbio where he worked at a leprosarium caring for the sick.

"Then one morning, riding past San Damiano on my way to visit a tenant farmer, I spied him. He was piling roof tiles that evidently he had removed from the church. A coarse tunic, held by a leather belt, covered his spare figure, and half-ruined shoes were on his feet.

"As I dismounted, he looked up at me, smiling a welcome, and said: 'Bernardo, have you come to help me for a while? With two of us I won't have to keep coming down from the roof. I'll pass the tiles to you, and you pile them here out of the way so they'll not get broken.' He spoke as though he had been expecting me.

"'All right, Francis,' I answered. And that's the way it has always been with Francis and me, Angelo. Even if we might not see each other for a long time we seem to pick up our friendship, even our conversation, it seems, at the point we were last together.

"So I said to him, 'You've decided to do the repairs yourself, then?'

"'Yes, Bernardo. I learned enough about masonry when we rebuilt the city walls a few years ago to be able to do this. But sometimes I need help. As I told you, God wants this done, so he'll send whatever help is needed. He sent you, didn't he?'

"I had to agree that he was right. We had worked for maybe two and a half hours when Father Guido, an old priest the bishop had assigned to the care of the church, appeared and offered us something to eat. Francis came down, we washed our hands in a bucket by the well, and sat down to share the bread and sausage that the old man had brought us.

"'I have to stop this,' Francis said.

"'Stop what?'

"'Stop depending on the priest for something to eat.'

"'I think I remember hearing some Scripture once, that "a workman is worth his hire." You're working here for nothing, aren't you?'

"'Yes, but I shouldn't make a practice of depending on him. He's poor. It will be hard, but after this I'll go up to the city and beg when I'm hungry. Maybe I'll come to your door, Bernardo. Would you give me anything?'

"'I might. But tell me, what are we taking the tiles off the roof for? If it leaks why not just replace the broken ones?'

"'Because we are going to add a second story to this part of the building.'

"'We are? It's plenty big enough already. There's only Father Guido, and he doesn't even live here. He has a house in town.'

"'I know, Bernardo, but it's not for Father Guido. One day there will be holy women living here. Nuns. It has to be big enough for them. You'll see.'

"'Holy women? ("Holy smoke!" I said to myself.) How do you know that?'

"'I don't know how I know that, Bernardo. I just know it. Isn't that strange?'

"'You're right, Francis, that's strange. And where are you going to get the stones you'll need for the second story? Are you going to go from door to door begging for them, too?'

"But any sarcasm was lost on Francis. 'Exactly,' he said. And didn't he do just that? I heard that he had borrowed a cart from someone and he went from house to house asking if they had building stones he could use for San Damiano. 'One stone, one prayer I'll say for you,' he would cry. 'For two stones, I'll pray twice for you.' And people would actually give him stones!

"It proved too much for his father, who happened to come to the square from his shop one afternoon just as Francis was passing through. 'You want stones?' he hollered. 'You want stones? Here's a stone for you, you crazy idiot!' and he hurled a rock in his direction. Then he broke into tears, turned and ran back down the alley to his shop.

"Francis stood for a moment looking after him, then continued on. 'Give me a stone,' he cried. 'A stone to rebuild San Damiano.'

"That evening I was at home. Concetta had cleared away the supper dishes and gone home when there was a knock on the door. I unbarred the door, opened it, and there stood Francis.

"'May God give you his peace, Bernardo.'

"'And to you, too, Francis. Won't you come in?' He stood there for a moment on the step, hesitating, then from behind his back where he had been hiding it, he held out a bowl.

"'Would you,' he began, 'would you, for the love of God, have anything you could give me to eat?'

"'Come in,' I said. 'Let's look and see if Concetta left anything in the pantry. She prepared some pigeons this noon and I ate only one. There should be another there.'

"There was. And some peccorina cheese. I put it all out, with some bread, on the table, and motioned to Francis to help himself, which he did. Then, taking his bowl filled with pigeon, cheese and bread, he went over by the hearth where the fire was still burning brightly, and sat down on the floor, the bowl in his lap. I sat on a chair at the table. Blessing himself, he said quietly: 'I thank you, Lord, for the food you provide through the kindness of Bernard. Please bless him and his family.' And looking at me, he said: 'Thank you,' and he began to eat.

"'I passed the house twice,' he said, 'before I could make myself knock at the door. Even so, I waited until Concetta left. Her mother works for my mother, you know. It's easier to beg from people who don't know me or the family. But that's my pride holding me back, so I forced myself to come to your door.'

"'Francis, I don't understand why you think you must beg for your food. If you don't want Father Guido cooking for you, maybe he could ask the bishop to give a salary for your work, then you could buy food you like, even if you had to cook it yourself. Or you are welcome to eat here with me. Why do you beg?'

"'Thank you, Bernardo, but I believe that God wants me to live as his son lived. Jesus didn't have money, did he? Someone else had charge of the purse to provide what was needed. Judas. And we know that for money he betrayed Jesus to death. No, if I had money I might be even worse than Judas. Nor did Jesus know where his next meal would come from. He accepted invitations or ate what others provided for him. I don't want to have a secure meal provided every day when our Lord did not have that. He didn't have a Father Guido to look after him.'

"'Nor did he have a place to lay his head,' I reminded him. I thought he looked a bit guiltstricken at that unfair remark. 'Where are you staying?' I asked.

"'At Father Guido's,' he admitted. 'He said I could stay in a spare room at the back of the church.'

"'Why not sleep here tonight? It's dark out and it's beginning to rain a little. I'll let you take some blankets and you can sleep here by the fire.' I thought that the suggestion of such Spartan comfort might encourage him to accept. It did.

"'All right, Bernardo. You're more than kind.'

"I have to admit, Angelo, that I was not sure about Francis. I was not, as I said, an intimate friend, but I knew enough about him to think that he was superficial, responding to the whims of those around him. Although I was impressed by his rejection of his father's money and his simple life at San Damiano, was he only playing at being a penitent? Was he looking for admiration and acceptance? Was this a serious change in Francis Bernardone or just a pose? So I spied on him that night.

"I started to yawn and suggested that it was late, that he must be tired, and perhaps we should retire for the night. Francis quickly agreed and made ready the blankets on the floor by the hearth. I got into bed and pretended to go at once to sleep, snoring a bit, but I could watch Francis. Not long after I started to snore, giving the impression I was asleep, Francis took off the blanket that covered him, got on his knees, and that is how he spent the night. Perhaps I drifted off to sleep sometimes, but every time I looked toward the hearth, he was still there, on his knees. At times I thought I heard a whisper or a sob. Finally, toward dawn, Francis lay down again and I guess he slept, until the clap of horses' hooves and the rumble of carts over the cobblestones told us the workers were going out to the fields for the day.

"That convinced me, Angelo, that what Francis did in daylight came from what he did at night, from prayer. And I was right, as you know. There was no pretext. He was not playing a role for anyone's pleasure, but to please God. He tried to live as Jesus lived, do what Jesus said we should do. It was as simple as that.

"The next week I went to San Damiano more often, and for longer stretches of time, to help Francis with the work. When we became tired, or when a shower came up, we would sit under the porch of the church and talk. He was interested in knowing about the crusade and my experience with the Muslims I had met. I wanted to know what led him to begging for his food and rebuilding a tumbled-down church.

"One afternoon we were sitting on the floor of the church waiting for the rain and the hailstones that hammered on the tiles above us to subside. The large crucifix that hangs there still at San Damiano was over our heads. Francis was gazing up at it when he said: 'Bernardo, do you see how the artist has pictured Jesus there? He has painted a few dabs of red, a hint of blood. But it must have been far worse than that! And do you see how the artist did not portray for us the anguish and pain that Jesus must have felt? A painting can give us only height and width, I know, not the dimension of depth. Just so it seems to me that we miss the dimension of Jesus' humanity: the poverty of his birth, the hunger and exhaustion of his life, the sorrow of his passion, the pain of his death and, yes, the joy of his Resurrection. The Jesus I want to know is human, as well as divine. When we overlook his humanity, to stress his divinity, we lose something of our own worth. I want everyone to have a true affection for Jesus as a brother and a friend. Perhaps then we will appreciate one another as brothers and sisters, adopted into his family, the Trinity.'

"That night he once again came to my door and begged for something to eat. Once again he stayed the night, and once again, pretending to sleep, I observed him as he prayed. The next morning we went to Mass together at the Church of San Nicolo. After Mass, as we were about to step out into the sunshine beginning to flood the Piazza Comune, I put a hand on his arm and I said aloud what had been welling up inside of me for days: 'Francis, what should I do with my life?'

"'Bernardo, I'm not the one to ask. You have to ask God that question.'

"'I've been asking, praying, but I'm as confused now, even more, maybe, than I was weeks ago. Since I returned from the crusade, I suppose.'

"'We can ask God to put it into words for you, Bernardo, if you want,' he suggested.

"I didn't know how he would get God to do that, but I nodded quickly in agreement.

"'Come on then,' he said, and steered me back into the church and down the aisle to the altar where the priest was extinguishing the candles.

"'Father John,' Francis said to him, 'could you show us please a Bible?' The priest went into the sacristy and returned with a large Bible, which he placed on the altar.

"'Now,' Francis said to me, 'say a prayer, Bernardo, asking God to tell you what he wants you to do. To yourself.'

"So I closed my eyes and prayed fervently asking God to make clear to me what his will might be. As I said, it was more or less a prayer I had been saying for weeks.

"When I opened my eyes Francis placed the Bible in front of me. 'All right, close your eyes again, Bernardo, and open the Bible.' I did so. 'Now take your finger and put it down on the page,' he instructed. I circled my hand over the opened Bible and put the point of my index finger on the page.

"'Open your eyes and read what you have your finger on.'

"I looked and saw I had opened the Bible to chapter nineteen of Saint Matthew's Gospel. My finger pointed to verse twenty-one.

"'Read it,' Francis urged.

"'*Jesus said to him, "if you wish to be perfect, go sell your possessions, and give the money to the poor, and you will have treasure in heaven; then come, follow me."*'

"'You asked, Bernardo,' Francis said, and he turned and walked down the aisle and through the sunlit door to the square, leaving me there at the altar, my finger still pointing to the words God spoke to me.

"'Now wait a minute, Francis,' I hollered after him and ran down the aisle and out into the square. I caught him by the arm. 'I can't do that! I can't make a decision like that just because of a line in the Bible that you open to by chance!'

"'By chance, Bernardo? Do you really think there is such a thing as chance? But you might be right that we are not giving God enough opportunity to express himself. Come on, let's go back.'

"We went back into the church and up to the altar where the Bible lay open as I had left it. Francis picked it up and handed it to me. 'Now, pray as you did before, but this time we will ask the Holy Trinity to tell you plainly what you are to do. We'll open the Bible two more times.'

"I closed my eyes and prayed again, opened the Bible and, as before, put my finger blindly on the page.

"'Well,' Francis urged, 'what does God say this time?'

"I opened my eyes. I had opened this time to the Gospel of Luke, chapter nine, and my finger was on verse three: 'Take nothing for your journey,' I read. 'Wow, Bernardo,' Francis whispered, 'you were right to ask for a clearer message. You can't get much clearer than that! Now, open it once more in the name of the Trinity and let's see what the entire message is.'

"I was glad, Angelo, that Francis had told me to pray to myself, because I changed my prayer around a little, asking God to be gentle with me."

"And was he?" I asked. "What was the third passage, Bernardo?"

"The Bible opened to Saint Matthew again, but chapter sixteen, and I had my finger on verse twenty-four."

"What did it say?"

"God told me, as he told you and told every one of us: 'If any want to become my followers, let them deny themselves.'

A gust of wind breathed through the foliage over-

43

head, a peaceful sigh. "And then? What did you do then?" I asked.

"Then," Bernardo replied with a shrug, "I did what Jesus told me to do. It wasn't easy, particularly dealing with my family, but in a week's time I was able to sell my property or give it away to the poor people I knew. Concetta helped me with that. Then one day I asked Francis to help me give away the money I had. 'Gladly,' he laughed. So on Saturday, market day, Francis helped me give away coins to anyone who put a hand out. Everyone thought I had gone crazy, of course, like Francis, but for some it was like a sacrament. The giving of the money brought grace: certainly to me, but also to those who took it—Sylvester, for example. He is Sister Clare's cousin, you know. He was a canon at the cathedral and his family is well off. Well, he happened by when Francis was giving away my money, and didn't Sylvester have the gall to come up and say that he thought Francis owed him money for the stones that he had given him for San Damiano! And Francis gave him a fistful of coins. Enough for a whole wall! But for Sylvester it worked like a sacrament. He couldn't get over it that I had sold everything and given it all away. Within a year he joined us, and you know what a fine friar he is."

"That's the end of the story, then?" I asked.

"No, that's the beginning of the story, really. That was when I joined Francis at San Damiano and together we worked to rebuild that church. Together we begged for our food up in Assisi and at the farms around. It was hard, so hard to beg for something to eat from former companions and even from people who once worked for me or still worked for my family. After a while I got accustomed to it, but even now it is difficult for me. Francis made a game of it, which one of us received the larger piece of sausage, the most eggs. That made it easier. Often we would work for our food on the farms during harvest time, rather than beg. It was hard, Angelo. Sometimes we had nothing to eat but some bread, nothing to drink but the water that bubbled up in the olive grove across the road from the church. And yet I was content, at peace. I had given away any security I had, made a fool of myself in everyone's eyes, I'm sure, and yet at peace."

He stopped and, caught in the memory of those days, looked off through the trees sloping down the mountain's flank in front of us. Sunlight, casting golden splotches here and there where it seeped through the oak leaves, illumined an occasional bee as it went toward the hives on a terrace above us. "Yes, that was a time of peace, Angelo. If we had stayed with the stones and cement, things would have been different, I'm sure. A few others came: John the Simple, we called him; and Giles, and Peter Catanii of course. Then we moved on to the chapel of St. Peter of the Thorn to rebuild that, and Philip joined us, and Angelo Tancredi. We went off to preach repentance to the farmers and townsfolk over in the Rieti Valley. That's when you met Francis and Giles and came to join us. Finally Francis arranged with the Benedictines up at San Benedetto to rebuild St.

Mary of the Angels. That is when things started to change, Angelo, once we finished repairing that little church. You were there. You saw it happening."

"How, Bernardo? What changed?" I demanded.

"Our purpose. Our purpose changed. What we did. I remember the exact moment, Angelo, that Francis (or God, who knows?) sent us in a new direction. We had been repairing our little church down there, St. Mary of the Angels. Oh, those were the days! Like Adam and Eve, we had little to wear and hardly an apple to eat, yet it was paradise. We were wretchedly poor, yet we had such good times together. When we finished our work on the church, replacing the last cracked flagstone in the floor, Francis suggested that we celebrate by having a Mass said in the renovated church. He asked Leo, ordained hardly a year, to say Mass for us there. You remember. Leo had been dropping by to visit us from time to time and to bring us food from people in the parish where the Bishop had assigned him. It was the feast of Saint Mathias, I remember, because the Gospel for the feast was our Lord's instructions to the apostles to go out and preach, to have no money, and so on. I have to admit it, Angelo, ashamed though I am, that my mind was more on the good job we had done with the roof than with the Gospel. And anyhow, I am not very good in Latin. But neither was Francis. So after Mass he asked Leo to read the Gospel again and to explain it.

"When Leo explained that Jesus was giving instructions to the apostles about going out to preach and how to live, Francis shouted: 'That's it! That's it! That's what I want to do!'

"And that *was* it, Angelo. From that moment on we did not rebuild another church. We became preachers. Granted, not like our cousins of the Order of Preachers, but just the way we lived, just walking along a street, should be a sermon for those who see us, Francis used to say.

"So from then on Francis used to send us out, two together, to the towns and farms around Assisi to preach repentance. I enjoyed it, Angelo, I admit, but I was too shy to be a good preacher. Preaching to the farmers was something we did only now and then. Mostly we stayed at home, prayed, and worked at rebuilding a church. No, I preferred the peace and quiet of the way we had lived before. I preferred to work with my hands, the feel of wood and stone and earth, and to see something done when I finished. More and more I would come up here to the caves to avoid the distractions of going out to preach. There were others like me. Sylvester up there, for one. But that is how you became a friar, right? Francis and someone...."

"Giles," I reminded him.

"Francis and Giles went out preaching in Rieti."

I nodded.

"And you heard them, saw them, and you came to join us."

"Yes," I admitted. "I don't think I would have been attracted by the rebuilding of a church, Bernardo. My hands do better with a lute or a violin than with stones and wood and tools."

"Perhaps not. But you know what I mean. Not everyone has the talent to preach or to deal with people. Someone has to stay home and pray, I think. That is what I have always wanted to do, and Francis was content to let me do that. The time is coming soon, though, when I will be joining Francis."

"Coming for all of us, Bernardo. We are getting long in the tooth. The younger friars have their own way of doing things, so let them go at it, I say. God is in charge, anyhow, so they can't do much damage. As for me, I just want to revisit some places hereabouts and find some old friends, to dig up some memories and brush them off."

"There's no going back, though, Angelo, is there? You know that."

"You're right, of course, Bernardo, but I think I have to go back, as best I can, before I can go forward. For several years now I have been living, in my spirit, if not in my body, in a time that doesn't exist anymore. I can't do that. No one can, or should, do that. So I want to say goodbye to those places, those times, and move on. Maybe like you say you are ready to do, with Sister Death. But the past has to be a place where the future sets its roots. It's not a place to put both feet; only one, as the other foot steps ahead to the unknown. So, dear friend, keep me in your prayers. I remember you always with great affection and will pray for you."

Bernardo struggled painfully to his feet and we hugged each other. Then I turned and followed the path that would lead me to the mule track that zig-zagged its dusty way down the mountain to Assisi. Actually there are two paths that go from the eastern gate that opens into the older part of the city, one that rises steeply that requires strong legs and heart for the climb up Mount Subasio to the hermitage, and the other that, as I said, wanders among the forest oaks and comes to an olive orchard beside the smaller fort. Cyclamens, their pink flowers blooming among the fallen leaves of the stone oaks, and daisies crowding together in the islands of sunlight scattered on the sea of shade under the trees, reminded me that spring was still struggling to free itself from the winter's cold. The path, moist and cold under my feet, came out into an olive orchard.

A stone's throw away from me, off by the city wall, someone was working among the trees, loosening the soil under the trees with a mattock. He had his back to me, but I could tell that he wore a friar's habit although he had it tied up around his waist. There was something, the way he set his feet, the way he swung the mattock, that seemed familiar. As I came near him, he paused to rest and must have heard me and turned around.

"Giles," I said, "is it you?"

"If I'm not Giles I don't know who else I might be. Who are you?" He was squinting his eyes against the sun.

"Angelo. Angelo of Rieti. Have I changed so much, have I become so old that you don't recognize me?"

"Angelo! I'm sorry." He pumped my arm with callused hands, giving me a grip that told me he was still strong. "If you had your lute strung on your back like you used to, I would have known you right away. It's my eyes, Angelo. They're not as good as they used to be. And in the bright sun everything is blurred. It's so good to see you! At least to see what I can of you. It has been ages since I saw you last. Are you at one of the houses here now? St. Mary of the Angels, maybe? You're not living at the tomb, are you?"

Some of us called the church and the friary where Francis now lay buried "the tomb." It was a cynicism among ourselves, a private joke, that it was the tomb not only of Saint Francis but of the Order as well. "No, Giles, I'm not staying anywhere. Just this morning I came over the mountain, stopped at the hermitage to see Sylvester and Bernardo, and now I'm on my way into the city. I don't know where I'll stay. Where are you living?"

"Down at San Damiano. Some of us older friars stay there to help out Sister Clare and the other Poor Ladies: Marico and Barbaro. They go out to do the begging, God bless them! I do that if I have to, but I prefer still to work for my food, as long as God gives me the strength. You know how I am."

I nodded. Giles was always a bit different from the rest of the friars. He was a young man when he came to Francis and asked if he could join with him and the others. One of the very first, right after John the Simple, Bernardo and Peter Catanii. Giles came from a large family of hardworking peasants whose farm was adjoining one of the properties that belonged to the Bernardones down in the valley near Rivotorto. He was a small, wiry man, hard as a hickory stick, accustomed to working with his hands and impatient with anyone who did not keep busy. Although he had no education, he was very insightful and took some delight, I think, in giving his observations on life. His "sayings" became popular among the friars, so much so that some have been collected and whenever we gather someone is sure to share one of Giles' latest.

"Whom are you working for here, Giles? These olive trees don't belong to the Poor Ladies, do they?"

"The Poor Ladies? They don't own the house they're living in! Not as long as Sister Clare is alive! No, this property belongs to the Tancredis. One of the brothers of Angelo Tancredi, our friar, hired me as a favor. He'll pay us with some oil when they harvest the olives in November."

The bells from San Rufino began to tell the angelus. Other bells, from convents I didn't know, took up the call to prayer. Out of habit we prayed the angelus together, once again thanking God for the gift of his Son through Mary. As the sound of the bells died away Giles said: "You can't have had anything to eat, Angelo, come and share what I brought with me. I have plenty. Some bread, a little sausage and cheese. No wine, though. I'm sorry. I never drink it."

"Thank you, Giles, I'd be glad to have something to eat. I haven't had anything to eat since early this morning, and I guess I used that up climbing over the mountain."

"Come on then, we'll sit under that tree over there where I left the water jug and the sack. I haven't dug around that tree yet."

We sat cross-legged in the grass under the tree and gave thanks for the simple meal God provided for us. When we had made the Sign of the Cross, Giles said: "Now tell me, Angelo, what brings you back to Assisi? To tell the truth, I'm surprised to see you. I thought I might never see you around here again."

"Well," I admitted, "I have been in no hurry to come back here. When Brother Elias started to collect money for Francis' tomb, I was glad to leave and stay away. The idea of collecting money in the name of Francis, after he had taught us to despise it, seemed repulsive. But a lot of water has gone under the bridge. I have been feeling the need to return to Assisi and visit once again, maybe for the last time, the places and the people that were part of those days when I first came over the mountain with Francis. Do you still remember that?"

"Of course I remember. I left you two at Spello and went to see my family, then we met again at St. Mary's."

"I was just speaking with Bernardo, Giles, about the old days, 'in the beginning,' as he says. It must have been a hard existence for you. Was it?"

"Angelo," Giles laughed, "if someone walks well in the way of the Lord, he does not feel tired or bored, but in the way of the world he feels tired and bored to death. Yes, life then in those early days of the Order was hard. But life itself is hard. It was hard for Jesus, the Son of God, so who are we who have asked to follow after him to expect that life will be any easier? Hard, yes, but those days were never dull, nor are any days dull now when we try to live like Jesus.

"I remember, Angelo, one of those expeditions when Francis sent Bernardo and me to preach conversion and penance to the people of Florence. We were full of vinegar, ready to convert the world. At least I was! Bernardo never did care too much for preaching, but I could hardly wait. We got as far as Passignano when we started to run into trouble. Around here people knew us and respected us. But farther north no one had heard of us. They thought we were crazy heretics. Just outside of Passignano we met some smart-alec kids who started to throw stones at us. Bernardo got between me and them to protect me from the stones. Then I got on the other side to shield him, lest he get hit. I got one stone off the head that made me see stars, I can tell you, but Bernardo didn't get it. We took to our heels and got out of range, but that was the way it was, Angelo, we looked out for each other. Outside of Sienna we got pelted with horse manure, and some men who had been drinking grabbed us and dragged us around by our hoods like sacks of flour. No, it wasn't easy in those days, but no one could say life was boring!"

"What kind of reception did you get in Florence?" I asked.

"Nobody roughed us up, but we weren't welcomed

by anyone, either. When we arrived we had no place to stay, of course, so we looked around. We walked by a house where a woman was sweeping the walk. 'Bernardo,' I said, 'let's ask that woman if we can stay at her house. She looks like a nice person.' He nodded, so I went up to her. 'Excuse me, madam,' I said, 'but I can see that you are a good Christian lady. We are Penitents from the city of Assisi, come here to preach to the citizens of Florence. God would repay you if we could stay at your house tonight.'

"She looked us up and down, and I think she smelled us, too, because we had been pelted with the horse manure, and I still had a big knot on my head where the stone had hit me. 'My husband is not at home, so I can't invite you to stay here,' she said. 'However there is a porch in the back where you could spend the night. It's covered. The oven is there and it's still warm because we baked bread today. You can stay there if you want.'

"'Very well,' I said, 'it will be better than sleeping under the stars. Thank you.' But it wasn't much better, Angelo. The weather had begun to turn cold, so Bernardo and I spent the night snuggling up to that oven as best we could to stay warm. I don't think I slept a wink, thinking of the comfortable home I had left, even if poor, to lie like an untrusted dog in the ashes of someone's back porch.

"In the morning we were up and off to the closest church we could find to say our prayers and to hear Mass. Bernardo is a great one for prayer, as you know, and I like to have time to spend with the Lord, too, so we must have been there quite a while when some gentleman came up to Bernardo and said: 'Pardon me, Brothers, I see you have been praying here for a long time and have attended Mass devoutly. Yet even though you are unmistakably poor, you haven't bothered any of us by asking for alms. Who are you?'

"Bernardo, who is better than I am with words, told the gentleman who he was, that he was himself a gentleman, but both of us had given away whatever we had and were followers of Francis of Assisi, trying to live poorly as Jesus had commanded.

"When the man asked us where we were staying and if we had eaten, we confessed that we had no place to stay and had eaten nothing so far that day. He then pressed us to stay with him and invited us to join him for something to take away our hunger. So we accepted his invitation gladly, staying with him and his family for several days while we preached to the citizens of Florence in the squares."

"What kind of sermons would you preach? You hadn't really been to school, had you?" I demanded.

"No, you're right. I'm not educated, really. So I just spoke about things I thought they should know, things that are common sense. I would say things like: 'If you want to see well, pluck out your eyes and be blind. If you want to hear well, be deaf. If you want to walk well, cut off your feet. If you want to work well, cut off your hands. If you want to love well, hate yourself. If you want to live well, die to yourself. If you want to make a good profit, know how to lose. If you want to be rich, be poor. If you want to enjoy pleasure, afflict yourself. If you want to be secure, always be afraid. If you want to be exalted, humiliate yourself. If you want to be honored, despise yourself and honor those who despise you. If you want to have good things, endure evil things. If you want to rest, work. If you want to be blessed, desire to be cursed.' And the people listened. They still listen, Angelo. People want to know how to please God and how to do what is right. A really bad person is rare. Most 'bad' people are simply overcome by some evil that they don't recognize or know how to overcome. No sinner should ever despair of God's mercy as long as he lives. For there is hardly a tree so thorny and knotted that men cannot make it smooth and beautiful. Likewise there is no sinner in this world so bad that God cannot adorn him in many ways with grace and virtues.

"Those must have been great times, Giles," I nodded.

"Oh, they were, Angelo. But they were hard on us, too. Sometimes I would be so hungry my stomach thought my throat was cut. I remember those days when I first joined Francis and we were living at St. Peter of the Thorn in Rivotorto. We tried to outdo each other in penances: the chains around our bodies, the hair shirts, fasting and praying for hours at night. Do you remember? But Francis cautioned us to be prudent in the way we dealt with Brother Body. Strict but prudent." I nodded, remembering how he forbade me one time to wear a hair shirt under my habit, saying I should be more gentle with Brother Body, while I was sure he had on a hair shirt at that very moment.

A fly had been alternately buzzing around my head and then lighting on the piece of cheese that Giles had shared with me. I swatted at it again. "What was the story about Brother Fly, Giles?" I asked.

He smiled a bit, shaking his head. "Soon after I joined Francis there was another fellow, about my age, from Assisi, who came to join us, too. Francis welcomed him. He knew the family, tradesmen. I think he had been studying law in Perugia, but he never finished his studies. When it was time for work, he either wasn't around or he was not feeling well. When we went out to beg, he asked Francis not to send him because he was ashamed to do it. But the man could eat! He ate enough for two. And he considered himself a fine preacher. One time, when he was going to go to Bastia to preach I couldn't resist saying to him 'Boo, boo; you talk a lot, but little you do.' I was sorry I said it, but it was the truth. Well, one day when we had been working on the Church of St. Peter and this brother had sat in the shade watching us because he had a sore back, he suddenly felt a lot better when Peter Catanii came back from begging some food and it was time to eat. Francis took the man aside, but I was close enough to hear him say: 'Brother Fly, go away. You eat up what the others work for and you do nothing to help. Go away.' All of which reminds me, Angelo, that I have work to do. The devil finds mischief for idle hands. Where are you going?

What are your plans?"

"I have no plan other than what I told you: I want to be in touch with the past again before I let go of it forever. I suppose I will go down to St. Mary of the Angels. There are a number of friars there I would like to see again."

"Before you go there, Angelo, come to us at San Damiano. We have room for you, and Sister Clare would be delighted to see you again. You would cheer her up, I'm sure; especially if you sang some of the songs for her that you used to sing for Francis when he was ill there before he died."

"All right, Giles. That's a good idea. I had hoped to see her. How is she?"

"Not well. She hasn't been very well for a long time now. But she is still the strong-willed woman you remember; she doesn't give in to her poor health. I'll plan on being back there by Vespers. I'll see you then."
With that he got to his feet and went back to work.

Inside the gate, I turned to the right and followed the narrow street to the path that led up the hill to where the fortress stood, unchanged, since I had first seen it several years ago. Never a very formidable fortification, it had been reduced to rubble by the citizens of Assisi back in 1198 and much of the stone used to reinforce the city walls. Francis used to tell of the haste to finish the work lest the Duke of Spoleto send troops to reclaim his rebellious town, or Perugia take advantage of the power vacuum and claim Assisi as its own. Walking around to the front of the fort, I surprised some stray goats that darted away through the shattered gate. The sun, at its zenith, felt good on my shoulders as a breeze rose from the valley below. There, seated on a large stone tumbled from the wall behind me, I looked out over the city and the valley. The city seemed much the same. A few new homes, perhaps, and the piazza in front of the cathedral seemed larger than I recalled, suggesting that perhaps some homes had been torn down to open a larger area. A burst of pigeons rising from the Piazza Comune drew my attention there and I wondered, idly, if Francis' brother, another Angelo, still had the family cloth store just off the square. I would have to stop by there, just to satisfy my curiosity. But my attention was drawn farther to the right, to the huge church built to honor God and the man people now called *Saint* Francis of Assisi. I had to admit it, it was impressive. Doubly impressive that it was put up in just eight years after his canonization and only ten after his death. Brother Elias, the head of the Order at the time, moved heaven and earth to bring it to completion. But agree with him or not, it wasn't all his doing. The pope had insisted, so there was no alternative, really. So there his body lies, somewhere buried in that mass of stone; just where, no one but Elias knows for certain and he is long dead, beyond telling anyone. But his spirit, the heart of my friend Francis, is buried nowhere. If one can bury a spirit, I would say it was at the little chapel of St. Mary of the Angels off there in the distance among the live oaks. But his spirit is free, unfettered and uncontainable. What does it matter where his bones and ashes are? The spirit of the man I knew, of the saint I called my friend and brother, is throughout this city and this valley, and I meant to find it.

CHAPTER

❧3❧

"WHO WAS SAN RUFINO?" I had asked. Francis and I stood in the square that November day looking at the unfinished church in front of us. We had just come through the gate that gave onto the track leading up to the Carceri where we had just come from, and then continued on to the Abbey of San Benedetto. The narrow street now emptied here at the piazza in front of the cathedral. Around us were the sturdy stone houses of the rich and behind us more homes with heavy shutters, some with towers, which bordered the piazza and the street. Family forts.

"You never heard of our patron saint?"

I shook my head.

"He was the first bishop of Assisi and a martyr. The Romans, pagans, killed him, because he refused to give up his faith and worship a pagan god or goddess. I don't know. Anyhow, he was a true Assisian: stubborn. And he has stood by us for hundreds of years, stubbornly protecting us, sometimes from ourselves. They whipped him, stoned him, threw him in a furnace, and then, with a millstone around his neck, threw him in the river. But he wouldn't give in, so they killed him, finally, with a sword. In the end, the soldiers who killed him and the proconsul who ordered it, all became Christians. This is his city and he keeps us in order until the Lord comes again. Stubborn."

"We are all stubborn here, Angelo. Proud. There are two main parts to the city. There's this part, the upper part, around the cathedral and behind us, the oldest part of town, called Saint Mary of the Roses, which goes down the hill to the main square, the Piazza Comune. This is where the old families, the rich and powerful people of the city have their homes. As you see, they live in homes like forts because over the years there has been a lot of violence, fighting, killing. They are good people, but fierce and unforgiving. They like to be called the *maggiori*, the 'somebodies.' Over there on the left, the second house from the cathedral, that belongs to the Offreduccio family, and next to it, the Scipiones. Two brothers. Across the way over there, the house of the Tancredi family. All of them basically good people, but they tend to think of Jesus as someone who leads them to victory in a battle, not as the good shepherd. The other part of town is made up of tradesmen for the most part, like my own family; and new land holders. They live in the lower part of town: the other side of the Piazza Comune and to the north. We call ourselves the *minori*, the 'lesser folk' or sometimes the 'new people.' Sometimes there is a lot of friction between the two groups, people trying to be in control. The bishop has his residence down in the *minori* part of town, and his church is St. Mary Maggiore, and yet the cathedral is here among the *maggiori*. Sometimes the bishop and the mayor have disagreements about repairing the cathedral here, the celebration of San Rufino's feast day, and so on. Then other people get involved, take sides, and there's trouble. Come on, let's go into the cathedral and say a prayer at San Rufino's tomb."

Inside it was cool and the frescoes on the walls obscure because the narrow windows, mere slits, serving better as a fortress than a cathedral, let in little of the sun's rays. Thick columns held up the rounded arch of the ceiling, a simple and austere building in the Romanesque style. Beautiful in its own way.

Francis led the way to the main altar where he knelt, and I followed, on the bottom step. A couple of candles, left by some hopeful friends of the saint, sputtered on the top step in front of the altar, their flames dancing in the draft from the windows. The altar itself, a large slab of marble, lay upon what appeared to be a Roman sarcophagus, decorated with nymphs and wreaths. "Saint Rufino's bones are in there, under the altar," Francis whispered. "Let's say a prayer that he will continue to bless Assisi and keep the citizens at peace." And he fell silent.

While he was praying my attention wandered from Saint Rufino and I looked about. The side altars, one dedicated to the Virgin Mary, I was sure, were hidden in deep shadow. In front of one of them a patch of shadow, darker than the darkness around it, seemed to move a bit.

From the darkness came a soft voice, a woman's:

"Francis?" Her voice echoed slightly in the stillness.

A woman, dressed in black, a black shawl over her head, emerged from the darkness. She was small in stature, slight, and moved as one full of energy.

"Mother, is that you?" whispered Francis, getting to his feet and peering into the shadows.

"Yes, Francis. I've just been praying to Our Blessed Mother for you and I asked her to let me see you. These days I never know where you are."

"Angelo," Francis said to me with some pride and affection, "this is my mother, Lady Pica di Bernardone. The world's finest mother and the best maker of almond cookies I know. You didn't bring me any, Mother?" Francis asked, kissing her and looking for any packages she might have.

"No, dear," she sighed, patting his arm, "I didn't know you would be here, and besides I didn't dare. Your father keeps an eye on me all the time. The only time I can get away is when I say I'm going to church. How are you? You look so thin. Have you been eating the way you should? Oh, excuse me, Messer Angelo, I *am* pleased to meet you, but I get so concerned about Francis here, I forget my manners. I'm sure he doesn't take care of himself, now does he?"

I nodded and shook my head, as best I could, at the same time, acknowledging her greeting and wanting to give her the answer she expected. "I'm pleased to meet you, too, ma'am," I said. "I'm sure I'll be seeing more of you."

"Angelo," Francis murmured, "why don't you wait

64

for me outside in the sunshine where it's warmer. I want to talk to my mother, but I'll be right out."

"Of course," I agreed, saluted Signora Bernardone, and retreated to the front of the cathedral where I took a seat in the square, by the watering trough, in the warm November sun.

It must have been a good forty-five minutes later before Francis emerged from the front door of the cathedral and, looking around, came over to me where I was feeding some pigeons with a bit of bread I had left from breakfast. He sat down next to me with a deep sigh.

"God is good," he said. "You probably guessed, Angelo, that my father and I are not on the best of terms. In fact we're not on *any* terms. I've been a disappointment to my father. He's a good man, really, but he is a businessman and a true Assisian: stubborn. He wanted me to take over the family business: dry goods. I wasn't interested and I had no head for making money. Then he wanted me to be a knight. The Lord had other ideas for me. He might have been able to swallow my becoming a proper monk, like those at San Benedetto up there, but here I am a beggar who, praised be God, like Jesus, is without a place to call home. Not only am I a disappointment, I'm an embarrassment for him. If we meet in the street, he avoids me or curses me. So he forbids Mother to have anything to do with me, forcing her to be devious, to run into me by chance as she did today. I want with all my heart to be at peace with my father, but at present I don't see how it can happen. Of course, for God everything is possible, so I leave it in his hands."

I could almost feel the ache in his heart, and I thanked God for the good relationship that I had with my own father, and threw some more crumbs to the pigeons who had settled once again around us. "Want some crumbs?" I asked, holding out some to Francis to share with him. "They are too fearful to take them from my hand, but if you throw the crumbs slowly, careful not to startle them, they will come pretty close."

Francis took some in his hand and sitting back against the water trough, cupped the hand in his lap. "Brother and Sister Pigeons," he said softly, "come!"

At once several of them fluttered to his lap, settled on his arm and helped themselves to the crumbs in his hand. Another perched on his shoulder, awaiting its turn to be fed. "I know you are not truly doves, but you are cousins, members of the same family, so I'm sure the Lord had you in mind, too, when he told his apostles that they should be innocent, like you."

Other pigeons, paying absolutely no attention to the crumbs I offered, a dozen or more in all, flew to Francis and settled on him. With his free hand he held two up in front of him and continued to speak to them, as a grandfather might to small children. And like children or dutiful students, they looked up into his face, intent on what he was saying to them. "You know what that means," he continued. "Simple and virtuous, and without guile. You should not envy the lark for his song, nor the swallow for its quickness. No, you should keep busy collecting food for your young and in the morning when the sun comes over the mountain soar as a flock to wheel over the city to welcome a new day. And in the evening, as the shadows spread across the valley, all of you should climb high in the sky for a last look at the sun before it falls below the mountains in the west. Now go, show me how you will do it." As one they rose into the air around us, clapping their wings like applause, and circled high in the sky above us, where they spiraled in a graceful dance before plummeting to the bell tower above us.

"Beautiful," Francis hollered up to them, as he clapped his hands. "Thank you! Didn't they do that nicely for us, Angelo?" he asked, turning to me. I had to agree that they did.

The sound of the pigeons, cooing in the bell tower above me, drifted down like feathers from the nests they must be building. The main door of the cathedral creaked, bringing me back to the present, and an elderly priest, a thatch of white hair on his head, stooped and walking with the aid of a cane, came hesitantly into the sunlight. He looked familiar. He was shorter than I, and I am not a large man, but he was sturdy of body like the ancient oaks of the forest on the mountainside above the city.

"Don Fabio?" I asked. I startled him for I was directly in his way and, momentarily blinded by the sunlight, he peered up at me through bushy eyebrows. His eyes were as black and bright as I remembered them.

"Brother Angelo, is it? Of course it is! How are you? It's years since I saw you last, at La Forresta, when you were there with Brother Francis. Excuse me, I should say *Saint* Francis, shouldn't I? Everyone knew, even then, that he was a saint. That's why all those people kept coming to see him, to see a saint. You saw how it was."

I nodded, seeing in my mind how it was. We had cut across the mountains, following the ox cart roads and mountain paths to the Rieti Valley. Brother Elias, he whom Francis had picked to replace him as head of the Order, had prevailed on Francis to go to Rieti where Pope Honorius was staying at that time with some of the cardinals. The Holy Father had offered the services of his own physician and was anxious that Francis would avail himself of the good man's skills. His eyesight was getting worse, so that he was not only almost completely blind, he was in great discomfort from the sun's light and the constant weeping of his eyes. Four of us accompanied Francis: Bernardo, Leo, Sylvester and I.

The treatment, when I learned what it would be, chilled me through with dread for Francis. The doctor prescribed searing the temples of Francis' head with a white-hot bar of metal in the hopes that this would dry up the flow of tears which the doctor presumed to be the cause of the loss of sight. Thinking back on it, I still shudder. The doctor sat Francis by the hearth and explained to him what he intended. I could see that Francis was afraid, but he gathered his courage and he spoke to the fire burning brightly in the fireplace: "Brother Fire, merry and strong, I urge you to be gentle with me. I put myself in your care."

When the doctor touched Francis' head with the bar of iron, searing him from ear to eyebrow on both temples, the room was filled with the smell of burnt hair and flesh. But Francis did not flinch; he gave no sign of pain at all. When it was over he turned to the fire and said simply: "Thank you, Brother." Those of us with him had more tears in our eyes than he.

People, hearing that the *poverello*, the little poor man, was staying in their city, came to the home of Teobaldo Saraceni, where he was staying, making it impossible for Francis to get any rest from his wounds and life became unbearable for the family. So at Don Fabio's invitation we fled to his little parish, St. Fabiano, outside the city.

It being a poor little country parish, the pastor supplemented the few coins that the parishioners could offer him by keeping a vineyard, making wine and selling the wine. He built, behind the church, a small stone building. In one half of it were the winepress and the barrels where he stored the vintage. The other half he offered to us as a place to stay, for it had a hearth where we might cook our meals. Francis, however, elected to stay in a cave in the rock shelf on which the building sat so as to have more solitude, the privacy it was ever more difficult for him to have during the last few years of his life.

When the news got out that Francis had not gone

far, crowds began to gather in the hope of speaking with him, asking for his prayers, perhaps receiving a cure. Men and women, the poorest and the richest, gathered around the church and on the priest's property hoping at least to get a glimpse of Francis. Although it wasn't yet time for the harvest, being only the end of September, nonetheless the grapes were ripe in the priest's vineyard. Such a pleasant spot tempted some to take their ease among the vines and, while they waited to catch sight of Francis, to help themselves to the grapes and even take bunches home with them when they left.

Poor Father Fabio was distressed at the people's abuse of his property, but also at the prospect of having no wine for the coming year for himself nor to sell. Although he did not want to complain to Francis about it, Francis learned of it and asked him: "Father, how many barrels of wine do you usually get from your vineyard?"

"Thirteen," was the answer.

"You will get at least thirteen barrels this year, too," Francis promised him. "In fact, if you get less than twenty I'll make up the difference myself. I feel responsible for your concern and the nuisance you've suffered. Now don't worry anymore and trust God to take care of you." Well, God wouldn't be outdone. Don Fabio was blessed with twenty-one barrels of wine—the best, he claimed, that his vineyard had ever given him.

"Yes, Father," I agreed, "I saw how it was. And how

is it now? Are you still getting wine from those old vines?"

"I'm sure I don't know, brother, but I doubt it. Those vines must be long dead, worn out by now. Anyhow I'm not there anymore, you know. I live right here in Assisi with my sister. Too old to work anymore, the bishop told me. He gave the care of the place to you friars. Didn't you know that?"

I shook my head.

"Yes, you friars are there now," he said again. "It is no longer a parish church, but many people go there to attend Mass and to pray and to speak with the friars. A place of peace in a crazy world."

After Father Fabio continued on his way, steadying his shuffling steps with a stick, I stood for a moment in the warm sun and looked around the square. Francis, as a young man, only recently converted to his life of poverty, used to stand on the back of the stone lion guarding the church door and from here preach to the people after Masses on Sunday mornings.

The sound of a shutter opening caused me to look up. A servant girl was putting some bedding out to air, hanging it from the window. It was the home of the Offreduccios, I knew, the family of Sister Clare. One of her brothers owned the house now, I'd heard. Perhaps that was the very window from which Clare, still a young girl, used to peek out to see who was talking to the people. And, seeing Francis, listening to his simple words, found herself wanting to be as free as him.

The door through which she crept out into the darkness of a Palm Sunday night so long ago had been closed up, I saw. The house remodeled a bit. She had arranged with Francis that she would meet us at St. Mary of the Angels, so she came, accompanied by her aunt, lighting their way with lanterns down the rutted road from Assisi. She was determined, she told us, to be a bride of Christ and to live in poverty as we did. Francis let her, there in the church that we had rebuilt a few years earlier, make her promises to be chaste, to live in poverty and to obey him as her superior for the building up of the Church and for her salvation. As a sign of her new way of life he took scissors, cut off her long blond hair and gave her a nun's veil to cover her head.

Years ago that was. Many a Palm Sunday have come and gone, and still Sister Clare is struggling to be poor. In her convent at San Damiano she and her sisters are still badgering the pope to give the permission to be poor: to rely on the goodwill of the people to provide.

"Better to have enough land to grow what you need," he cautions. "Better to own some properties and have the rent as a secure income," he says.

"Better yet to rely on the God who makes the olive and the grape grow, on the King to whom all creation belongs," she replies.

I'll have to go down to San Damiano to visit her, I decide, as I pulled open the cathedral door and entered into the shadowy coolness. Standing in the back I looked toward the main altar dappled with dim sunlight from the window slits above, as it was that

November day years ago. Another elderly woman, this one as old as an olive tree, was moving with arthritic slowness, arranging a bouquet of flowers. She turned her face, pale in the frame of a black shawl, toward the sound of the closing door.

"Who's there?" she asked. And straightening as best she could, she motioned me closer. "You're one of the brothers, aren't you? What's your name?"

"I'm Brother Angelo, Mother."

"Angelo Tancredi?"

"No, Mother," I said. "I'm another Angelo. From Rieti."

"Oh, I know you. Don't you remember me?"

"No, Mother," I admitted. "I'm sorry, but I surely don't. The light is none too good in here," I offered, drawing closer to see her better. "How do we know each other?"

"I'm Olimpio's mother. Brother Olimpio," she smiled, and the church seemed to brighten. "You have to remember him! Don't you?"

And indeed I did. Olimpio Crimi was barely sixteen when he came to us, a slim boy with a shock of unruly blond hair and a ready smile. He was her only son, her only child, but he wanted to be a friar, so she would consider herself and her husband blessed if we would accept him, she had said. They were a very poor family. Ottavio Crimi, the lad's father, was a tenant farmer down the valley near Spello. Indeed, as it turned out, Giles knew them and vouched for the boy.

Olimpio was a gem, a credit to his mother and

father. Although good-humored, he was serious about being a virtuous friar and gave much time to prayer. It was shortly after his period of probation and taking his vows, that his father died in a harvest accident. Some months later Signora Crimi came to St. Mary of the Angels looking for Francis. It was more from a need to talk to someone, I think, than from any expectations of help, but she poured out her story. After Ottavio's death, she had been forced to leave the tenant farm for she could not do alone the work expected of her. She had no place to go but to a married sister who lived in Spello, who took her in. Her sister, too, lived in great need, having several children and married to a stone-mason's assistant. An extra mouth to feed soon brought the whole family to the edge of homelessness. Olimpio, now stationed in Perugia, could not help and she did not want him to know.

Francis asked her to wait a moment and he called all of us together. He told us of Signora Crimi's plight and asked: "What can we give our mother?" He always called a friar's mother our mother for she had shared with us her son.

Francis looked at me, and I scratched my head. "What do we have that anyone would want except maybe the clothing on our backs?" I asked. The others, too, looked perplexed. After all, we had no money; that was forbidden by our Rule.

"Maybe we could send her to a friend, one of our benefactors, and ask for help," Bernardo suggested.

"No, Bernardo, she came to us, to her family,"

Francis murmured. A smile came to his face. "What about the new book of Readings for Mass that we received yesterday? She could sell that for a good sum!"

"But Francis," Leo objected, "we just got that, and we need it for Mass."

"We got along before somehow, Leo, and maybe God will provide us with another, but at this moment our mother is in need and that book seems to be of more use to her than to us."

So Francis pressed the book of Readings on her, and we heard later that with the money she got from it she was able to buy a few goats and sheep and support herself with the cheese and wool she sold.

"Saint Francis was a compassionate man," she whispered, as though reminding me. And he was that. Sometimes I hear a friar, usually someone who never lived with Francis, recount an anecdote of his life and I wonder if that could be the person I knew. He was strict, yes, but mostly with himself. He was not frivolous, but neither was he mirthless nor frigid, like a fresco. He enjoyed songs, denounced sadness, and had great compassion for those who suffered from the weight of our human condition.

There is a story the friars tell of their early days together living in the narrow shed at Rivotorto. They had just returned from Rome, having obtained the Holy Father's blessing to live in poverty and do penance. Lest I embarrass the friar, I will not mention his name, for he was carried away in his zeal to do penance and deny his appetite. After having fasted for several days, he awoke in the middle of the night and found himself sobbing: "I'm dying. I'm dying of starvation."

The commotion, awaking everyone in the wretched hovel where they were crammed in like toes in a tight shoe, Francis took him by the arm and, leading him outside, took him to a nearby vineyard where he commanded the friar to eat grapes and in the future not to abuse his body to extremes. When they returned and the others discovered what had taken place, they all commenced to cry: "I'm dying of hunger! Give me some grapes or I'll surely die!" So, with some elbowing and giggling they all went out to the vineyard, shared some grapes, and had a good laugh.

I must have smiled at the memory, for Signora Crimi smiled, too, and asked: "Have you seen my son recently? Seen Olimpio?"

I shook my head.

"He's a grown man, of course, and has a lot of duties. He's the superior there in Perugia now, you know. The guardian they call him. So he will be coming to St. Mary's for the chapter meeting. I'll get to see him, and make sure he's eating all right. One never stops being a mother, you know," and she gave me another smile and, reaching out a hard, worn hand, patted me on the arm.

She reminded me, as I said, of an olive tree on the mountainside where I had seen Giles. She, like the tree, had seen many difficult times, had sunk her roots deep into the earth of Umbria; had produced fruit; had prevailed.

"God bless you, Mother," I whispered, and turned to go.

"Thank you, Brother Angelo," she said. "May he bless you as he has blessed me."

CHAPTER
❧4☙

A S I SAID PREVIOUSLY, the upper, older part of
Assisi holds the homes of the *maggiori*, the titled
and more prosperous older families. The Blues, they
call themselves. Some of the homes date back to
Roman times. In the lower part of town, the more
recent, live the Reds. These are the *minori*, the trades-
people and laborers. During the May holidays the two
rival groups meet in jousts and competitions, for the
most part friendly, and there are also musical and
poetry contests. What joins the two parts of town
together, a common meeting place, is the main square,
which boasts the town hall, the ancient and columned
temple of Minerva, a fine fountain and some shops. In
the evenings it is a place for the townspeople to gather, at the end of the day, to drink a glass of wine and
share any news before going home for supper. Later,
after supper, the square belongs to the young unmar-
ried men who gather to sing songs, tell jokes and play
their games.

I remembered the square well from those years
before I was a friar, for I had come to Assisi during the
May holidays to enter the ballad competition. What a

marvelous time I'd had, singing and playing far into the night, not only with the local youth but also others like myself who had come from as far as Sienna and Florence.

Coming down the street from the cathedral and into the piazza, remembering that night years ago, a figure, a face, suddenly stood out in my mind. Strange, I never considered it before, but I could remember now a young man, slightly built, expensively dressed, who was the life of the party. He went from group to group, leading them in song, laughing, calling to this one and that of his friends. Francis! When we met at Rieti some few years later, he, dressed in a ragged and patched habit, his hair cropped close to his head, I had not recognized him, although there was something about his bright and penetrating eyes, his quick gestures, that stirred a faint memory.

Leaning over the lip of the fountain to cup with my hand some water that flowed down from Mount Subasio, I drank and wiped my hand over my face a few times to rinse away the dust. Then I turned to the left and entered the street that would bring me out of the town by the western gate to the path through the olive groves to San Damiano and Sister Clare. Before me, shuttered and silent, sat the Bernardone house, Francis' home. When Francis was a young man, it was a gathering place for other youth, always sure to find something to eat in Lady Pica's kitchen, a welcome from Pietro Bernardone, if he happened to be at home, and some entertainment brewing in Francis' fertile mind.

I knew, of course, about the falling out Francis had with his father. When Francis left home, publicly declaring that from then on God would be his father, if Pietro Bernardone was ashamed of him. In his hurt, his anger, his pride, Francis' father would verbally abuse him when they met by chance in the streets of Assisi, and to his business associates would declare that the beggar they would see in the streets was no longer a son of his, but a mad fool.

Did they ever reconcile? In February of the year he was to die, Francis had been very ill. The dropsy he suffered from had become worse and he was in constant torment from his eyes, which had now become almost completely blind. Also, he was in pain from the wounds the Lord had shared with him. Brother Elias, the superior of the whole brotherhood, arranged for Francis to go from the little hut at San Damiano where Sister Clare and the other Sisters had been caring for him, and to stay with old Doctor Quattrone in Assisi. Brothers Giles and Rufino and I helped care for him.

One evening Francis and I sat on the floor near the hearth. Although he could not see it well, he liked to be close to the fire for the warmth, but also he found in the dancing flames and the crackling of the wood, evidence of the merry personality of Brother Fire. A flaming coal jumped out of the hearth with a pop and landed on the edge of the cloak I had wrapped around Francis. He sat there and watched it come to flame and burn the material, but he made no move to shake it off. If I hadn't done so, I know that he would have let it burn the cloak and perhaps himself as well.

"Brother Fire, so strong and merry, has a big appetite," he said simply. "Appetites, Angelo," he continued, "are what govern us. Some are good, lead us to God and happiness, and need to be encouraged; others are bad, drive us down a road away from God to misery, and these we must pull out like weeds or closely govern. My father had an appetite for wealth and the esteem of men. Those appetites directed his whole life. And I have to admit that for much of my life I had the same appetites: acclaim, the good life that wealth can provide, a life free of care. But then God blessed me with a year in prison, a year-long view of my life from a dungeon; and then a year of illness when I almost died. Yes, God blessed me, Angelo, and took away my appetite for those things that had been so important. In their place, he whetted new appetites in me: for simplicity, for humility, for a heavenly kingdom instead of an earthly one. And those appetites were directly opposed to my father's. He no longer understood me. I was suddenly a stranger to him. And I was no longer attracted to his values nor to his hopes for me. It was difficult for both of us, Angelo. He was sure I had lost my mind, I guess, so convinced was he that happiness and worth lay in getting rich and having everyone's respect.

"God was teaching me that the way of happiness depended on 'putting on the Lord Jesus Christ,' as Saint Paul says. That meant embracing poverty, as God himself embraced it, emptying himself to take on our flesh;

suffering rejection and trials, and yet loving and forgiving everyone; picking up whatever cross God provided and following in the footsteps of Jesus. The old appetites of pride, laziness, selfishness were at odds with the appetite I felt to imitate Jesus in every way. So they had to be rooted out, disciplined. You remember how hard we worked to change our lives."

I nodded and sighed, remembering the hours spent in prayer; our suffering from the cold in winter; the pain of hunger gnawing at an empty stomach.

The red coals of the small fire in the hearth gave Francis' face a color that belied his sickness. He spoke slowly, his voice weak, remembering. "It was early April. A few weeks only after Peter Catanii's death. I had only given over the governing of the Order to him the year before and now he was dead. A dear, dear friend he was, Angelo, and I felt that maybe the fault was mine: that if I had not put that burden on him he might not have died. He took my place out of obedience to me. I was alone that day in the Church of St. Mary of the Angels, sitting on the pavement next to the wall. On the other side of the wall we had buried Peter and carved his name on one of the outside stones to mark the place. I lay my head against the cold stone, my ear against it, listening to the stillness of Peter down there in the earth below the wall. It was the stillness, the quiet, not of absence, as when no one is there, but the stillness of presence, as one experiences before the tabernacle in an empty church.

"'Peter,' I whispered to him, 'I miss your strength

and your wisdom. Thank you for being such a faithful friend and brother. Now do me this last favor. Do not work any miracles for the people who come here to pray at your grave. Do not subtract any splendor from our Lady.' As I spoke, I heard the door behind me open and someone enter the church. Slow footsteps, uncertain on the uneven pavement, stopped beside me.

"'Francis?'

"I looked up and standing beside me was my father. Even then my vision was not good, Angelo, as you know, but in the dim light I could see well enough that he had aged considerably since I had seen him last a few months before, at a distance, in the square. He had lost weight; his clothing hung on his frame. He had a walking stick to steady himself and I could see that the hand that held it trembled a bit.

"'Here, sit here,' I said, pointing to a bench by me. He lowered himself to it and leaned back against the wall. The outline of his face against the light of the sanctuary lamp was that of an old man. How much like my grandfather, I thought. 'Are you feeling all right?'

"'Your mother would give me hell if she knew I had escaped her,' he sighed. 'She watches me like a hawk, afraid I'll do too much. All right? No, I am not all right. I'm sick. Sick and old. All of a sudden I'm an old man. But I had to come down here, Francis. I wanted to visit Peter Catanii's grave, for one thing. He was a good lad growing up. And I guess I was hoping that I would see you, too. Giorgio Catanii, Peter's father—he and I have always been friends. We grew up together. He and his wife were by the shop yesterday. They're broken up, of course, that their son died, but at the same time they are at peace with it. They have a lot of faith, those two. That started me thinking. If someone came and told me that you had died, how would I take it? What would it mean to me?

"'For a while, after you left home, after all the trouble we had, it was as though you *had* died. When you took off all the clothes you were wearing that day in the bishop's courtyard and said in front of everyone that I was no longer your father, that God was, I felt that you had died. I was angry, angry and hurt and ashamed. Sometimes I wished that you *were* dead. At first everyone laughed at you, said you were insane, and I knew they were laughing at me, too, the father of the town's madman. But then things began to change. People began to admire you, tell me what a fine man you were. And that hurt almost as much, because I had this anger in my heart, and maybe I had somehow misjudged you, mistreated you.

"'Such hopes I had for you, Francis. I had been fortunate in the business, had worked hard, could provide you with opportunities that I never had. You were the oldest son, my heir. And you turned up your nose at it. How could you choose to be a beggar when you might have been rich? And yet, if you had become insane, why were so many people joining you? Peter here, Bernardo, Leo, the Lady Clare. They couldn't all be insane. And of course your mother. She would have gone off to join Lady Clare and the other ladies, too, if I

85

would have let her. She might yet,' he grunted, 'when I die.

"'Anyhow, I have come to realize, not too late, I hope, that I was not angry at you. I have been angry at my failed plans for you. I was angry that I could not make you into my image and likeness. Since I was a little boy working in your grandfather's wool shop, working long hours instead of playing as the neighborhood boys were, I promised myself that I would be rich. And if I had a son, he would be able to play and wear fine clothing and have plenty of money. I promised myself that.

"'Well, I did have a son. A beautiful son. He didn't have to work, he had plenty of time to play with his friends and he was popular. He was generous to a fault with his friends, had money to throw away. I didn't mind. It would come back one day, I figured, from these noble friends of his. But then he *did* throw money away, really, and he became someone I didn't know. He would throw money, money I worked so hard for, out the window to beggars in the street! He acted crazy! But now I think, now that life seems to be coming to an end, that I prefer the son you became to the son I had in my mind. Francis, my son, before someone comes to me to tell me that you have died, or before someone tells you that I have died, I wanted to set things right between us. If I did wrong by you, if I was too hard or demanding, if I gave you bad example as a father, I am sorry. Will you forgive me?'

"Tears were now running down his cheeks and he

was still enough of the man he was that he tried to hide them from me. I got to my knees and put my arms around him. I felt his hand, trembling a bit, on my head, as I lay it against his chest. Tears were running from my eyes, too, as I told him: 'You are my father and I guess we are more alike than different. If I have hurt you or caused you sorrow, I'm sorry, too. Forgive me, Father,' and I kissed his cheek.

"He kissed me on both cheeks, as he always used to do when he returned from his long journeys to France and Sienna and Florence to buy cloth. 'Well,' he said, clearing his throat, 'your mother will kill me for being gone so long. Pray for me and for her. And pray for your brother Angelo. He's not much of a businessman.' Getting up, he started painfully for the door, picking his way carefully over the uneven flagstones. 'You have two fathers, Francis,' he said, as he pulled open the door, 'me and God. Both of us love you.'

"'I have two fathers,' I repeated, sure that he heard me before the door closed behind him."

From the western gate a path sliced across the slant of the hill through the silvered olive trees. Around the trees the earth had been dug up, but in between and along the path crimson poppies mingled with yellow daisies. Off to the right some hives buzzed with bees coming and going, collecting pollen from the spring flowers. A small girl of no more than five or six, knitting some stockings and watching a dozen sheep, watched me go by, shyly looking away when I looked in her direction. Underfoot the dirt of the pathway was dry and the grass already showing signs of need for rain. It had been a dry spring, evidently.

Passing by San Benedetto, the farm belonging to the monks at San Pietro in town, I soon came out in front of San Damiano. It was just as I remembered it from that day years before when I left Assisi, determined that I would not return. I had stopped here to say goodbye to Sister Clare and the other nuns before taking the road to Terni and Narni, away from the rivalries and arguments that swirled around Assisi. And as I left, I had turned, stood here in this very spot, to fix the image of its poverty in my mind's eye, sure that I would never see it again.

What a peaceful place, I thought. It had seen dangerous and ugly days, as when Frederick II's Saracen mercenaries, besieging Assisi, had invaded the cloister. Sister Clare confronted them, armed only with the Blessed Sacrament of the Body and Blood of Jesus in a little box that she had one of the Sisters bring her from the chapel. "Lord, look after these servants of yours whom I cannot protect," she had prayed, holding the box out in front of her, facing the troops who had climbed over their walls. Miraculously, inexplicably, they turned and fled, leaving the Sisters in peace.

This is where we had brought Clare shortly after she had left home and determined to become a follower of Francis. He had first taken her to a convent of nuns of the Order of St. Benedict, a short way up the valley toward Perugia, in Bastia. Then to another convent of nuns closer to Assisi. But she was not content at either.

She had her own ideas of what type of life she would lead, that she would have nothing to do with benefices and estates, that she would live by begging, as the friars did, so Francis acquiesced and brought her here. And here, in the peace of San Damiano, the plant of religious life that she had planted took root and was flourishing.

Before long she was joined by members of her family and other ladies from Assisi and the area around. They became known as the Poor Ladies, a name that particularly suited Clare, because that, to me, explained her so well. She was a lady. Not just because she was of a noble family, but because of her character. Since I first met her as a young woman I had been impressed by her simplicity and her charm. Although she had a fine intellect and was possessed of many talents, she was completely unassuming and attentive to others, from the most crude peasant to the pope himself. Anyone who met her sensed that Clare was interested in their welfare.

Faintly, a bell tinkled. Afternoon prayer, Nones, I thought. The nuns will be assembling in their choir behind the little chapel to pray. As I stepped into the dim coolness of the chapel the lilting cadence of the hymn welcomed me:

Rerum Deus tenax vigor,
Immotus in te permanens,
Lucis diurnae tempora
Successibus determinans:
Largire lumen vespere

Quo vita nusquam decidat,
Sed praemium mortis sacrae
Perennis instet gloria.

Lord God and Maker of all things,
Creation is upheld by you.
While all must change and know decay,
You are unchanging, always new.
You are man's solace and his shield,
His rock secure on which to build;
You are the spirit's tranquil home;
In you alone is hope fulfilled.

I knelt down on the cold flagstones, alone in the little church, except for memories left here by countless souls, mine among them. The ponderous crucifix that had spoken to Francis, bidding him to rebuild this church that was in bad need of repair, still hung there over the altar. The face of Jesus, in repose now in his victory over death, looked down on me as it had on Francis. His eyes seemed to widen, as though asking me what I would pray for, what might it be that I wanted here.

What was it that had brought be over the mountain, back to Assisi, after such a long time away? Memories, I had said. But memories of what? In my heart, I knew: memories of the "true peace of heart" that I had known when Francis had been alive, a peace that was diminished and which at times altogether evaded my heart since his death. Here I could sense that remembered peace, as though it was lying, overlooked, forgotten as a discarded mantle, left in a dark corner of the chapel.

"When you spoke to Francis that day, Lord," I whispered, "giving him that task of rebuilding a church fallen into disrepair, he did not understand until later that you had the whole Church in mind. What you said to Francis had its effect in my life, too. In so many lives!

I looked around at the familiar church with its Romanesque arched ceiling and faded frescos darkened by years of candle smoke. Over there was the window which let in from the porch outside what dim light illuminated the interior. And there was the sill where Francis had tossed the purse of coins from the sale of his father's cloth in Foligno. When the priest here at San Damiano would have nothing to do with the money, fearing the wrath of Francis' father, Francis left it there and forgot about it. A dove, puffed up and cooing softly, strutted along the window sill and bowed before a prospective mate. Life goes on. With me or without me life goes on; there is no way to hold it back or slow it in its course.

The nuns had finished their prayers so I went to the grill behind the altar and pulled on a rope which jangled a small bell on the other side. Presently a viewing window slid open and a nun, her face covered with a veil peered out. "Praised be Jesus Christ," she said.

"Now and forever," I responded. "Good afternoon, Sister, would you ask Sister Clare if I might have a few words with her? I'm Brother Angelo."

"Brother Angelo! Don't you recognize me?"

"Recognize you! Sister, forgive me, but I can't even

91

see you under that veil! How do we know each other?"

"I'm Rufino's aunt. Sylvester's sister. Clare's cousin. You know, Sister Imelda!"

"Of course, I thought I recognized your voice," I lied. "What's going on here at San Damiano? A family reunion?"

"Just about, Brother Angelo. You wouldn't believe how many of us are related to one another. You want to see the abbess? She hates to be called an abbess, you know. I do it to tease her. She prefers being just Sister Clare. She is feeling better today and was in chapel just now. Let me see if she's still here. I know she will want to see you. Go around to the front door of the monastery, to the visiting room," she said, and slid shut the panel of the window with an authoritative click.

Clare had never been robust, and the difficult life she had taken on herself of fasting, midnight prayers, the lack of fundamental comforts, all of these had taken a toll on her meager health. Although frail of body, however, she was a fortress of determination. When she fled from her comfortable family home to join Francis' vision of imitating the poor Christ, she would accept no half-way measures. Like the woman who had ten coins, who could not bear the thought of losing one, of having "almost" ten. No, she would not be content with "almost" being poor, of "almost" imitating Jesus in his want. She withstood the advice of family and friends, of priests and bishop, of the Holy Father himself, and would not accept a way of life that was safe, secure, provided for. She would hear none of it. She wanted the privilege of poverty for herself and for her Sisters.

I found my way to the whitewashed visiting room, bare of furniture except for two cane-bottomed chairs facing a grill in the far wall. Around the walls, a few other mismatched chairs stood awaiting larger groups of family members who might come to visit one of the nuns. A work-worn hand pulled back the curtain behind the grill and there sat Clare. Her fair skin was taut across her cheeks, the result of sickness and fasting. She looked all of her fifty years, but her eyes, the same clear blue of the Umbrian sky in June, gave an indication of the iron determination that lay behind them. And yet, at their corners were the wrinkles of laughter and a quick wit. Leaning against her leg was a walking stick, a sign of her fragile health.

"Angelo?" she said, and she gave me a smile that brightened the room a bit.

"Yes, it's I," I admitted. "What do I call you? Abbess? Mother? Sister?"

"Call me Clare, Angelo, as you always did. We're of Francis' family, you and I. It's so good to see you! What brings you here after all this time? When you left here that day, shaking the dust of Assisi from your feet, I thought we would never see you again this side of heaven."

"I know. And I meant it, too. But things change. Time has a way of softening hearts. It did mine. How are you, Clare? It has been a long time since I saw you last."

"How am I? My health, Angelo? Not well. This is

93

one of my better days. I can't keep food down, so I get so weak that I can't stand up, let alone walk. But here I am, still alive, for as long as the Lord wills it. But how am I as *Sister* Clare? I couldn't be better! The pope still has not given me what I want, to live completely poor, but I'll never give up until I get his blessing. That is what keeps me alive, Angelo. Sheer stubbornness! But you didn't come to ask me how I'm feeling. Why did you return?" She looked into my eyes as though trying to see inside my head.

"I did come back because I wanted to see you again, Clare, to be able to see for myself how you look and hear for myself your voice. I have missed our friendship. It's hard to keep a friendship alive at a distance. And I came back to enliven my memories, Clare. Rufino, Leo and I are responding to a request that Brother Crescentius, the Minister General, made at the General Chapter last year in Genoa. He wants to compile an official chronicle of Francis for the whole Order. Your cousin Rufino has already given me some stories that he remembers, and so has Leo. Now I want to add to what they have written and put it all together. But I find that my memory needs to be renewed, so I've come back to visit old friends and places."

"And you want me to jostle your memory? Angelo, you lived with Francis, traveled around with him! You knew Francis far better than I. I never laid eyes on him except for once or twice when he still helped out in his father's shop, until he started to preach in the cathedral square, and I would listen to him from the window of my room. Remember, when the city revolted against the Duke of Spoleto, my family along with many others were driven out of Assisi. We went to Perugia and weren't allowed back until after that war when Francis was captured and spent a year in prison there.

"My older brothers were more his age, so they knew him better than I. At first most people thought that he was crazy, that the year in prison had put him over the edge. But when Bernardo di Quintevalle gave away everything he had and joined Francis here at San Damiano, people started to think differently of him. When my two cousins, Rufino and then Sylvester, joined him, my father was outraged at first, but they lived so poorly and were so sincere, that eventually even he spoke well about them and said the other clergy in town could learn a few lessons.

"My mother was slower to trust Francis' sanity because of what he did to cousin Rufino one day. Do you remember when he sent Rufino from St. Mary of the Angels to preach to the people in Assisi?"

I shook my head. "Not really," I said. "He often sent us off to preach somewhere, but always with another friar."

Clare nodded and, recalling the event, laughed as I remembered she often used to do. "It was a Saturday morning, market day, and mother had sent me with my sister Agnes to buy some artichokes because ours weren't ripe yet. We were passing San Nicolo Church when out of the door exploded Signora Crespi and a neighbor of hers. They never cared much for our family, ever since the town declared itself a commune. Anyway, when she saw me and Agnes she said: "Don't fail to see the preacher there in church, girls," and she laughed and winked at her friend.

"I knew something strange was going on, but I couldn't resist going in to look, so I took Agnes by the hand and in we went. There, in the pulpit, was cousin Rufino preaching to a handful of people. And he was dressed, or undressed," she laughed again, "in his underwear!" Rufino has a ruddy complexion anyhow, but his face was bright red, and he was stammering with embarrassment while he was encouraging the people to amend their ways and go to confession.

"Just then Francis darted in the door behind us, ran down the aisle and got up in the pulpit with Rufino. And wasn't he in his underwear, too! He put an arm around Rufino's shoulders and told everyone how he had sent Rufino to preach without his habit to test his obedience and to teach him humility. Then he apologized to Rufino and to all there for having done that. We were all moved to tears.

"Angelo, I thought then and there that I would love to be one of you friars. It seemed like such fun, and you were so joyous in the ways you tried to live the gospel, so sincere and honest. If I were a boy, I would have left Agnes standing there and followed Francis and Rufino back down the hill to St. Mary of the Angels.

"But I wasn't a boy. My parents were not oppressive about it, but they expected me one day to get married. *I* expected one day to marry. I hadn't thought a great deal about it, trusting that my father would arrange a marriage for me with a good man and I might even come to love him. But that Saturday morning was the beginning, I think, of a yearning for something beyond the horizon of marriage. Maybe I inherited a sense of adventure from Mother, who had made pilgrimages to Rome and even to the Holy Land, I don't know. It was a kind of itch deep within myself and I didn't know how to scratch it.

"The itch would be worse when I would catch sight of Francis or you, any of the friars, trudging up the street toward the Carceri or going on over the mountain to Gubbio, Ancona, I didn't know where, to pray in the forest or to preach. You seemed so free! Free to respond to whatever God asked of you. But I felt so confined by peoples', by my own, expectations for me."

"But look at you now, Clare," I said. "A nun! What could be more confining than your life here as a nun? Your whole life is within these walls of San Damiano!"

"Yes," she smiled, "it seems strange, doesn't it? We go out if we have to. The point is that we don't *want to* go out! There is nothing beyond our walls that interests us or that we can't help by our prayers. In here, Angelo, we are free. We are free to go over the mountain if we so desire, as you did, but we choose not to. We have another mountain to climb: the mountain of God. We're not bound by any expectations here but our own; the freedom one finds only in God is here. There is only one freedom we lack, Angelo, and that is the freedom to be utterly poor, as we promised God we would be. The pope will come to see it our way in time. I'm patient. I'm stubborn. I won't die until I have that permission, in writing, in my hands! You'll see!"

Clare moved uncomfortably on the chair. "Am I wearing you out?" I asked. "Perhaps I'm expecting too much of you, wanting you to remember long ago things."

Clare smiled wistfully. "You know better than I, Angelo, the things Francis did, what he said. What he said to me, was little enough. I used to beg, send messages, that he come and visit us, give us some instruction, encourage us in our lives as nuns. You recall how rarely he would come. He said he wanted us to rely on God, not on him, for guidance. It was hard, but that is what we learned to do.

"One Ash Wednesday he came to talk to us. We had gathered in the choir and waited eagerly for his sermon. Just to see him was a delight. Well, he came into the choir, but instead of preaching us a sermon on penance, as we expected, he sat down on the stone floor. We waited for him to begin, to say something, but instead he took out a sack he had brought with him and proceeded to sprinkle ashes on his head and all over himself. He sat there for a while in silence, then got up, and left!

"There wasn't one of us who was not weeping. It was the most powerful sermon on penance that I have ever witnessed. I'll never forget it, Angelo, nor forget the truth of his teaching that day. That is the way he taught us. His example was his 'words' to us. As they are for you friars, I'm sure."

"Yes, I know, Clare, but there must be a lot of things that happened, even miracles, that others will want to know about. He went to so many places, as you know. Some of those stories I probably never heard, and I'm sure there's much I have forgotten."

"Well, he almost deprived us of those stories, you know, Angelo."

"How so?" I asked.

"Shortly after he obtained the Holy Father's blessing for his way of life and was back here, living in that awful shed at Rivotorto, he must have been having second thoughts about what God wanted of him and you friars. You know how he loved nothing more than to go off to some deserted place to pray for weeks at a time. Should he give himself to that style of life, as a recluse, he wondered, or continue to travel about preaching to the people? So he sent Brother Masseo here to me, and then to Sylvester up at the Carceri, to ask us to pray to God to make clear his will.

"Angelo, I prayed, but it didn't take me an instant to be sure what was God's will for Francis! He was already spending great amounts of time in prayer, and he always would. Besides, what did he think we ladies were doing here at San Damiano, if not praying? What people needed was to hear the gospel preached, to see it lived in a courageous way. So I sent back word to Francis that God wanted him to preach. And didn't Sylvester send back the same answer as I? So that put an end, thankfully, to any indecision."

"Do you miss him, Clare?"

"Do I miss him? Angelo, that's a silly question! Of course I miss him. Does one miss the sun on a dark winter's day? But I have to tell you honestly, I often missed him more when he was alive than I do now that he is dead. He brought me here to San Damiano, encouraged me to be a nun, and then I wouldn't see him or hear from him for weeks, yes, months at a time. When I needed his advice, some encouragement, he left me alone. He was teaching me to rely on God and not on him, of course, but it was hard. Very hard. Now, of course, I know that he will not come one day to the door to give us a sermon or some instruction, but we have the example of his life, a few admonitions that he had Leo write down for us. So that's enough, isn't it? His few words, more, the example Francis gave us, they are a light in a dark place. Ultimately, of course, we have the Holy Spirit to guide us just as he did Francis. So yes, I miss *seeing* him, but Francis is as much a part of our lives here as ever he was."

Her eyes lifted over my shoulder and she smiled. Turning, I saw Giles standing in the doorway.

"Come in, Giles," Clare said. "You've finished work early!"

"Yes, Clare," he said. "Mount Subasio is wearing a crown of black clouds and it's starting to thunder, so I thought I would quit before I got soaked. Am I interrupting something?"

I shook my head, and Clare assured him: "No, not at all. Please, sit down and join us. We were just reminiscing about those days when Francis seldom came here to see me. If it hadn't been for you and John and a few others, we wouldn't have known a thing that was going on. And we might have starved to death as well, for you often brought us food you had begged."

"Oh, Clare," he laughed, "you nuns always knew more about what was going on in Assisi, and I'm sure in all of Italy, than the mayor and maybe the pope himself! People always felt sorry for you and wanted to be the first to let you in on all the secrets."

She smiled and blushed a bit, reminding me so much of the young woman I would see at San Rufino Cathedral with her mother or her aunt. "Giles, you have a bit of the devil in you," she said.

"Tell the truth and shame the devil, Clare," he replied with a grin.

"Speaking of the devil," I said quickly, seizing the opportunity, "do either of you recall any stories about Francis having any encounters with the devil?"

"Well, I don't know if you can call them 'encounters,' but I remember a few times when Francis was convinced that he was set upon by the evil one," said Giles. "And I believe he was, because I saw the results of the devil's visit. One time when Cardinal Leo Brancaleone invited Francis to visit him in Rome, Francis took me along as a companion. The cardinal had been very kind to us friars, helping us out in the very beginning of the Order, so Francis was indebted to him and longed to repay his friendship. When the cardinal offered Francis a lovely room in his palace,

Francis declined and asked instead to stay in a tower on the property where he would be able to pray and not be involved in the social life at the main house. The top floor of the tower was divided by about nine pillars into little alcoves, much like cells. Francis chose one; I went into another. I knew that it was his custom to spend much of the night in prayer, and I stayed awake quite a while, too, but finally fell off to sleep.

"During the night I was awakened by what sounded like a scuffle in the alcove where Francis was staying. Suddenly he was there beside me, shaking me, and asking me to light a candle. When I found an ember from the little charcoal fire we had used earlier to warm ourselves and cook some corn meal, I lit the stub of a candle. Its feeble light showed a shaken Francis, quaking with fright. He seemed to be covered with welts, bruises and bumps on his face and head.

"'Francis,' I cried, 'what happened? Who attacked you? And why?'

"'Oh Giles,' he moaned, 'it was the devil. He had been whispering terrible things into my ears, suggesting awful temptations to me, against my vow of chastity. The devil was in the pillow, I swear! I prayed and prayed, I called on Jesus to help me, I flung the pillow from me, against the wall, and then wham! bang! he started to beat me. There must have been an army of them, Giles! Would you mind if I stayed here with you?'

"'What if they come back, Francis?' I asked nervously. I guess I was afraid they might include me in the beating.

"'We'll pray,' he whispered. 'We'll pray to Saint Michael the archangel. God gives him much power, you know, over the evil angels. I should have thought of that earlier.'

"So that's what we did. We spent the rest of the night praying, and as soon as it started to get light, we left the tower and found our way to the cardinal's chapel. Francis was a sight, black and blue from the beating, one eye swollen shut. No one asked any questions and we didn't offer any explanations, but I'm sure there must have been some whispering among the servants who saw us. I've always wondered if they thought Francis and I had a disagreement between ourselves and he got the worse of the argument. Anyhow, we spent the next few nights in a room in the cardinal's palace until we left, and there was no more problem."

"That reminds me now of an incident like that, Giles," I said, "that happened at Greccio, where we had gone to spend the forty days before the Feast of the Assumption. And that involved a pillow, too. I didn't hear anything or see anything, but the morning after our first night there, Francis came out of the cell the friars had let him use and he handed me a pillow. 'Angelo,' he said to me, 'take this outside and burn it. Make sure not a feather escapes!'

"I thought I must have misunderstood him because you know how respectful he was of anything that people loaned him to use. He always took very good care of the thing and returned it.

"'Burn the pillow?' I asked.

"'Yes, Angelo, burn it. The devil is in it and he gave me a very bad time last night. I don't want anyone else to go through what I had to suffer. They might not be as fortunate as I. So make sure you burn every feather, lest the devil use it somehow to attack someone else.'

"The devil used to torment him when he was staying here, too," added Clare, "after he received the wounds of our Lord up there on Mount Alverna. But you two must remember! You were both here with him. Do you remember how we built a hut for him in our garden? His eyes were giving him so much pain and he couldn't bear the sunlight, so he stayed in the hut all day until sunset. The wounds in his hands, his feet, his side, gave him constant torment, but especially on Fridays. He was sick from dropsy, too, and unable to keep anything on his stomach. But besides the physical suffering that he bore, he was tormented by the devil. Francis swore that the devil tried to disturb his peace in every way he could: by sending mice which ran over his face, robbing him of any sleep; by whispering rumors to him of some of his friars who were more interested in honors and prestige than in simplicity and poverty."

"Well, he had cause enough to worry," Giles grunted. "It seems to me that the Order is going to hell in a handbasket."

"Not as long as you have anything to say about it, Giles," Clare laughed and winked at me. Giles had a deserved reputation for saying what he thought, to anyone, and without being asked.

He grinned and blushed a little, both pleased and embarrassed. "What's right is right," he asserted. "Our Lord said of himself that he is 'the way *and* the truth and the life'. We friars are quick to insist that our Rule, based on the gospel as it is, is The Way, and that it leads to Life. We are too quick to overlook that other ingredient, The Truth. Sometimes the truth is painful, but if we speak it, listen to it, and live it, then we are truly following our Lord."

"Don't despair, Giles," Clare said. "I understand your concerns for the Order and I know it must aggravate you to see the Order change from what it was when you came to San Damiano to join Francis in rebuilding this place, even before it became my home. But remember that Francis promised the Order would last. Friars like you and Angelo here will always be present to keep the past alive and open the door to the future. Our Lord had to walk a difficult road. That is the same road all of us, the Order, too, yours and mine, must walk. Difficult, but with Jesus and with Francis' example, easy. Angelo, do you recall the final verses that Francis composed when he was lying ill in the hut out there?"

I nodded, remembering.

"Let's sing them," she urged. "Like the old days." And we did.

Happy those who endure in peace, by you, Most
  High, they will be crowned.
All praise be yours, my Lord, through Sister

> *Death, from whose embrace no mortal can*
> *escape.*
> *Woe to those who die in mortal sin! Happy those*
> *she finds doing your will!*
> *The second death can do no harm to them.*
> *Praise and bless my Lord, and give him thanks,*
> *and serve him with great humility.*

We sat there for a moment, each with our own thoughts, remembering that part of our lives and the life of Francis. Those days seemed to have taken on a life of their own now. A part of our own lives, true, because we had a share in shaping them, but separate from us, too. They were moments like beads strung on the thread of time for anyone to count. I so wanted to put on paper those days for future friars and others to read. The story of any life is the story of God's actions in time. But nowhere, I think, is that more evident than in the life of Francis, Saint Francis of Assisi, my friend.

Clare slowly and stiffly, with the aid of her cane, got to her feet. We did also. "Will you be staying here tonight with Giles and the other friars, Angelo?" she asked. She had a faint smile on her lips, but I noticed that her eyes were about to brim over with tears.

I looked questioningly at Giles and he nodded, so I said, "Yes, if I may. I would like that. I don't think I am ready to go on to St. Mary of the Angels. Better tomorrow. It has already been a long day."

"Then sleep well, Angelo. You are welcome, of course, to join us at Mass in the morning. God bless you, dear friend, and good night." She reached up, released the curtain, and it fell, covering the grill.

As Giles and I came out of the monastery door I looked up the steep path that led to Assisi. The city itself was out of sight over the crest of the hill and behind the olive trees that covered its steep flank. But beyond, in the distance, I could see the top of Mount Subasio and, as Giles had said, it was covered with black rain clouds. Indeed I could see the rain descending down the mountain toward us like a curtain being lowered to bring the day to a close.

"Hurry, Angelo," Giles said. "Our little house is just down here to the left below the monastery wall. Hurry or we'll get soaked through."

We scampered down the steps that followed the line of the hill along the wall and arrived a step before the rain at the small porch that fronted the little friary that housed the friars who took care of the spiritual needs of the nuns. Giles showed me to a tiny cell with nothing more in it than a cot and a chair. The small window looked out on the fields and woods of the Umbrian Plain and there, not more than a mile away, St. Mary of the Angels.

Pulling the chair over to the window, I sat looking out on that part of the world that had been my home for many years. Rain fell gently, steadily. I could almost hear a sigh of contentment from the thirsty earth below the window as the acrid odor of the rain on the dry earth drifted into the room. There is something about the sound of rain on the tiles above one's head, the smell of wet earth that bring a sense of contentment and peace. That is what I felt at that moment looking out over the farms and cottages that Perugia and Assisi had fought to control for hundreds of years. Contentment and peace. Not that all was right with the world nor in Assisi. It wasn't. Not that San Damiano, St. Mary of the Angels, the Valley of Umbria gave a contentment not found elsewhere. They don't. But sitting there in that poor little room with the rain falling gently on the roof overhead and on the olive trees outside the window, I felt myself, I think, once again in the presence of the spirit and personality of Francis. It was that which filled me with peace and contentment.

It was on a night such as this, several years ago, that Francis and I sat together in the doorway of a hut on a small island in the bay at Venice. He had returned only a few days previously from the Holy Land. It was 1220. He and a dozen or so friars had gone off to Egypt to join the crusaders at Damieta the year before.

The soft patter of the rain did not drown out the measured sigh of the waves of the Adriatic as they lapped the beach of the island and receded down the sand and pebbles a few yards away. We sat there in silence together for some time, I with my thoughts and Francis with his.

In his absence he had left two friars to guide the Order and care for the friars. They had given in to the insistent demands of some of the more monastic-minded members of the brotherhood, had convened a Chapter, passed legislation requiring more frequent and stringent fasts and other innovations that would hinder the freedom that Francis believed the gospel gave us. Alerted by a friar who had sought him out in the Holy Land, Francis had returned quickly to take up again the leadership. However, he seemed a bit different. He had contracted an eye infection while away, which was causing him some difficulties, but more than that he seemed less inclined to press his views on others. Although a fire burned brightly in his heart, it was a fire to illumine those around him rather than to consume them. He had always been, since I had known him, a peaceful person; now he was a man of peace.

"It was an awesome experience being there in Egypt with the armies, Angelo," he had confided to me. "Thousands and thousands of men from all over Europe. The only things they had in common seemed to be that they were Christians, and they had come to kill Muslims. There were so many different languages that I could understand hardly anyone. Even the people from Italy spoke dialects that I had never heard before! You remember that we went over on a ship from Ancona, so I stayed pretty much with them and some others I discovered who were from Perugia. What a Tower of Babel it was! And the lack of organization added to the confusion. It seemed evident to me that that army was not about to win any war if the enemy was disciplined and prepared to fight.

"Going about the camps and talking with the soldiers it became evident to me that most of them were good and pious, but they had no idea why they were there in Egypt. They had joined the crusade to take the holy places back from the Muslims, but they had no idea who the Muslims were. They believed that the Muslims needed to kill Christians in order to get into their heaven; that they would invade France or England next if they were not stopped now; that they made slaves of women, killed all the men and kidnapped all children to make them Muslims. But I didn't know any Muslims, either, so I couldn't really say that they were wrong.

"So I said that it seemed silly to me to travel all that distance to wage a war with someone you really know nothing about. Let me go and meet these Muslims, I thought, and see what they're like.

"Angelo, they were very nice people."

"You met them?" I asked, for some reason surprised.

"Yes, I did. It was easy. I just walked out into the distance toward the Muslim camp until some Muslim soldiers came out of their fort and surrounded me. I couldn't have been very threatening, all alone, and you see how small I am. They searched me for a weapon, and when they were sure I had none, they escorted me into their fort. I couldn't understand them, of course, nor they me, but I knew the name of their sultan, Melek-el-Khamil, so I kept saying his name. And smiling. I smiled a lot! So that is where they took me, to see the sultan! He was a nice man, Angelo. We got along very well together. There was an assistant there who I learned had served in the army of Frederick II in Italy, so he translated for us.

"The sultan wanted to know, of course, why I had appeared on his doorstep, as it were, so I told him that I just wanted to meet him and his friends. I told him that I liked him very much, that he seemed to be a very wise man and ruler, and that he would be very much happier and sure of going to heaven if he became a Christian. I even offered to walk through a fire that was burning in the fireplace if his own religious leaders would accompany me. When the translator said that to the sultan, I saw some of the onlookers look worried. They must have been Muslim priests or something. But the sultan laughed and said that that would not be necessary."

"Well, what did he say?" I asked. "Did he become a Christian?"

"No, he didn't. But he might. He said he would think about it and I should pray for him to make the right decision, which I certainly do every day. But don't you see, Angelo? I don't think God wants us to *kill* the Muslims. That's not the way to convince them that they would be better off to be Christians! We should talk to them. We should become friends with them, maybe live among them. Our example would do more to influence them, and in the meantime we could live at peace, not at war. If the time were right, we could also preach to them. What is accomplished by war, by killing? I saw so much misery, sickness, such waste of time and effort during the months I was there.

"The Sultan had some soldiers escort me back to

our own area, where everyone was surprised to see me safe and sound. They seemed to take it for granted that I would be tortured, if not killed. So when I returned in one piece, and with a present from the sultan as well, they were amazed. After that I tried to prevail on the crusaders to try a peaceful settlement with the sultan and even told them that they would lose the war if it came to that. Some listened to me. We have quite a few recruits, new friars. After a few days the leaders of the crusade invited me to go visit the holy places and gave me safe passage to go there. So that's what I did.

"The rain, Angelo, as God reminds us, falls on everyone: the just and the unjust; the Christian and the Muslim, the young and the old, everyone. God cares for, provides for, loves each one of us. The water that touches our shore here tonight perhaps will wash up on the shore of Egypt tomorrow. God has given it to all of us. Who can say that it is his alone and no one else may use it? It makes no sense to me that we should quarrel with another, abuse another, any more than one child of a family should despise or abuse another child of the same parent. We friars, perhaps better than anyone else, should be willing to preach the message of peace and reconciliation to others. At least, Angelo, that is what I want to do."

CHAPTER
⇜5⇝

MORNING BROUGHT, as so often happens after a rain, a cloudless sky. After prayers and Mass, I set out for Santa Maria degli Angeli. It seemed, because of the clear air, closer than the mile or so that it was. Actually there was nothing to be seen from this distance except the woods where the chapel sat, and a few wisps of smoke that arose from the hearths of the friary, and perhaps a forge, to disappear in the cobalt sky.

"I'd like to come with you," Giles said, "but I have to finish the work in the olive orchard that I started yesterday. Will you come back here, Angelo, or do you plan to stay down there at St. Mary's?"

"I really don't know, Giles. I'll see what the Spirit offers me. If I'm not here for Vespers, then don't expect me."

The sun had risen above Mount Subasio and was warming the fields and the olive groves, as I walked down the path to the valley floor. Larks busily darted back and forth, reaping a harvest of insects for themselves and their young. Of all birds, Francis admired larks the most, especially the hooded larks, for they reminded him of friars. "Our sisters, the larks," he used to say, "do not peck around in the dirt for their food like other birds, but God feeds them while they are in flight above the earth, free of the mire of this world. Do you see how they dart up to the heavens and sing God's praises as they go about the work that God has given them? That is the way it should be with us. Even though we are bound to the earth, our hearts should soar free from cares and from sin."

I wondered what I would find there at St. Mary of the Angels. St. Mary's is more than a place. It is a state of mind, a way of looking at life; it is a vision of future hope and a summation of past joys. It is, if he had been able to say it of any place on earth, the spot that Francis called "home." It is from St. Mary's that he and we went off to preach the gospel; and it is there that we returned to enjoy our life together as brothers. I needed to recall some of the past moments of joy and to renew any vision of hope.

The closer I drew to St. Mary's, the closer I came to those events that were part of the past I wanted to touch again, if only in my mind, to savor those moments and see them from the present, to understand the importance of those past experiences in the light of where I was now.

The surrounding area looked unchanged. The same farmhouses: the Rosignolis', the Belias'. There was Primo over there in the field, hoeing among his artichokes, as I remembered him years ago. He looked up and I waved. He waved also, wondering perhaps who

I might be. 'No,' I thought, 'it can't be Primo. It has been too many years and he was elderly even then. Perhaps he was Luciano, his son. Good, hard-working people.'

It was Primo and his wife Rita who first brought some food to us at that Chapter back in 1221 and then alerted the other farmers in the area who likewise came with food for the friars who had come to the Chapter. Five thousand of us!

Even now, when the Order has grown far beyond that, I can hardly believe it. Five thousand friars came from all over Europe. In 1209 when we went down to Rome to ask the pope's blessing on our way of living the gospel there were twelve of us. Five thousand friars at the Chapter only twelve years later. And how many more were unable to come?

Honorius III was the pope and Cardinal Hugoline (who would succeed him as Gregory IX) was the cardinal Francis had asked to be the Protector of the Order. Francis had given over the leadership of the Order the year before, finding the task too much for his declining health, and had asked Peter Catanii to assume the duties of governing in his stead. And then Peter had died, less than a year later. Everyone, from the pope to the youngest novice in the Order sensed that this was an occasion of importance. So they came, five thousand friars, and cardinals, and bishops, and interested laypeople, not only to be present at the decisions that needed to be made, but also with the hope of seeing Francis, of perhaps touching him, of speaking with him, of obtaining his blessing.

Five thousand friars, plus dignitaries and onlookers—every house became a hostel, every barn a shelter. Every tree offered shade from the heat and perhaps protection from the rain. And how did all of these people eat? Some, of course, brought provisions with them. But most relied on the providence of God and God's providence took shape in the gifts of bread, vegetables and wine from the townspeople of Assisi, from the farmers in the valley, the neighbors of Primo and Rita.

What a momentous time it was. Most of the friars had only heard of Francis, had never met him or heard him speak. This was perhaps their only chance to see him, if ever they would, for it was general knowledge that his health was not good. We friars elected Brother Elias to be our Minister. I have to admit that it was with some misgivings, later proved to be correct, if I may say so, but Francis let it be known that he would be very happy to have Elias succeed to the position of Minister vacated at Peter Catanii's death. So, yes, we elected Elias. Francis would sit at Elias' feet as he conducted the Chapter and, when he wished to make known his thoughts, he would tug on Brother Elias' habit who would bend down to listen to Francis, then in his booming voice announce to the crowd: "Brothers, this is what Brother Francis says," repeating it for the crowd.

The Chapter was not only a gathering to do business and make decisions. It was a celebration of our way of life; it was an opportunity to renew friendships and make new friends among the more recent members; it was a sharing of the experiences of those who had gone off to preach.

As the Chapter came to an end, friars were sent to all parts of Europe: to Spain, France, Hungary and even to Syria. Some, hearing of the difficulties found in one nation or another, and of the possibility of martyrdom, were eager to go to the most dangerous areas, hoping to gain that reward. Friars who had been in Germany had the most harrowing stories to tell, of beatings and mistreatment by the citizens there; so many rushed to have their names included among those to be assigned there.

By the end of the Chapter it was clear to all that the power of Francis' personality and example, great as they were, would not suffice to hold the Order together in the future. It was becoming too large, too unwieldy. Some laws, some rules in writing were necessary. Pope Honorius said as much to Francis, so he complied at the end of the year and wrote a Rule for himself and the friars. What happened to that Rule, I can't say. It never found its way to Rome for approval. Some say that some of the friars who saw it thought it too difficult and were not in favor of it. In any event, that Rule was "lost."

So again Francis, in 1223, wrote another Rule. He went to Fonte Colombo, a poor little place among the rocks on a hillside near Rieti, taking with him as companions Brother Leo, who often acted as secretary and could say Mass, and also Brother Bonizo of Bologna, who was a canon lawyer skilled in the proper terminology. This Rule he did not give over to the care of

Brother Elias, who claimed to have lost the previous one, but gave it to Pope Honorius for his approval. I have the Rule imprinted on my mind and on my heart as clearly as it is printed on the parchment up there in the sacristy of the Church of Saint Francis on the hill. It begins: *"In the name of the Lord! Here begins the life of the Friars Minor. The Rule and life of the Friars Minor is this, namely, to observe the Holy Gospel of our Lord Jesus Christ by living in obedience, without property, and in chastity. Brother Francis promises obedience and reverence to his holiness Pope Honorius and his lawfully elected successors and to the Church of Rome. The other friars are bound to obey Brother Francis and his successors."*

At Fonte Colombo he composed the Rule which all of us follow even today, but it was at St. Mary of the Angels that we had lived that form of life before ever it was put into writing.

The hedge around the area of the chapel and the friars' huts, planted even in the days when I lived here, gave seclusion and privacy to the friars. I walked along the road which bordered the property, in my days no more than a rutted path leading up to Assisi, and gave a tug to the rope hanging beside the gate. A bell tinkled joyfully inside. After a few moments a smaller door, framed in the larger gate, opened and an old friar, as wrinkled and bald as a prune, stood there leaning on a cane.

"Praised be Jesus Christ," I said.

"Now and forever," he replied.

"Juniper?" I hazarded.

"You have the better of me, brother," he returned. "The voice sounds familiar, but my eyes don't see as well as they once did. What's your name?"

"I'm Angelo. Angelo from Rieti," I added. "What are you doing answering the gate?"

"Angelo!" he cried, dropping his cane and giving me a hug. "I'm so glad to see you, speaking figuratively," he said. "The truth is, I can hardly see you at all. To me, you're just a fuzzy shape. That's why I'm answering the gate. I had been assigned to work in the garden, but it got so I was pulling up the vegetables instead of the weeds, so here I am. So I can't truthfully say 'you look good,' Angelo. But listen to me talking away. Come in. Come in."

I picked up his cane, put it in his hand and followed him into the cloister, closing the door behind me. It pained me to see Juniper picking his way carefully ahead of me, slowed by his poor eyesight. My memories of him were of a small man quick in his step and in his movements. Small he still was, even smaller. But no longer abrupt, bird-like in the way he would flit from one undertaking to another. Over the years I have heard stories about Juniper that would lead one to think that he was simpleminded. Far from it. Juniper was indeed a simple person, literal in his manner of understanding life. But simpleminded, no. The story that the young friars love to tell, about Juniper cutting a leg from a farmer's pig, is true enough but it puts poor Juniper in a bad light. To Juniper's way of thinking, the farmer, wishing to help the friars and owing them for a day's work they had done to bring in the harvest, owed them as much as a pig might be worth. The friars did not need much, certainly not a whole pig, just enough of a pig to add flavor to their soup. The pig still had its life and three of its four legs, after all, and could get about quite well. So the clamor by the farmer and his wife puzzled Juniper, although he could understand the outcry by the pig.

In front of us was the little Church of St. Mary of the Angels. The door stood open.

"Juniper," I said, "let me go in for a while. I want to make a visit."

Juniper smiled and nodded. "I'll find a room for you," he said. "You'll stay with us for a while?" I nodded and he turned to slowly find his way past the church to the two-story structure that the city of Assisi had built for the older and sick friars, the one Francis had once threatened to demolish and where he had died.

"Don't leave me, Juniper," I said. "Come, sit with me, pray with me for a while." He turned and together we went into the little church where we had, with the other early companions, and with Francis, spent so many hours in prayer. We sat down on the flagstone floor, our backs against the wall, after we had reverenced the Blessed Sacrament.

"People say, Juniper, that there is no going back. Time goes on and yesterday is history. No one can live in yesterday. But here, in this church, Juniper, I am back. I am home. Rub the walls, Juniper. Do you feel the smoothness of the stones? They are worn smooth by our prayers and the prayers of countless others. Feel the smoothness of the flagstones. How many feet have shuffled across this floor? Feet from all over Italy and beyond, come here to follow after Francis as you and I did or maybe to receive God's pardon that Francis, at the Lord's request, asked of the pope. Do you remember, dear Juniper?"

"Yes, Angelo, I remember. I can barely see the floor, I can hardly make out the walls, but in my mind's eye I can see us here, as it used to be. And the faithful still come here to confess their sins and ask God for release from punishment. Yes, I remember."

"Do you remember, Juniper? Do you remember the lamb that someone gave Francis? We hadn't the heart to eat it for it took to Francis like a daughter to her father, followed him everywhere, and would pray with us here in church. Do you remember that lamb? Do you remember how Francis could speak to birds and they would listen, seeming to understand? The hawk that would awaken him to pray at Mount La Verna? The wolf at Gubbio that he gentled, the rabbit that would come to him and sit in his lap? Do you remember how it was with him and animals, Juniper?"

"Yes, I remember, Angelo."

"And the example he gave us, Juniper? He had nothing else to leave us or give us, he would say, except his example. Do you recall how one winter's day, tempted to give up his penances and prayers and live a life of common sense, he made for himself a wife out of snow, children out of snow and servants, and said: 'Now then, Master Francis, you had better get busy, if you want a wife and children and servants, for you have to feed them and clothe them.' Do you remember, Juniper?" And Juniper, I could see, was smiling and nodding his head as he remembered.

"And do you remember, dear brother, the time when, once again tempted against chastity, that he took off his habit and rolled himself in the rose bushes, leaving drops of his blood on their leaves as the thorns tore at his body? Even now the thought of it makes me shiver. Do you remember?"

"Yes, Angelo, I remember very well. Those rose bushes are still here and not a thorn grows on them now."

"And the evening he died? Do you remember, Juniper, how the larks swooped low over the roof of the infirmary there behind the church, as though they had come to gather his soul and lift it up to God with a song? I thought my heart would break that evening. It was as though a spell had been broken. Francis was gone, and all that remained was the emaciated carcass of a corpse. The spirit, the soul, life had gone out of him, Juniper, and we were suddenly alone in a cold and ugly place. I was afraid that the life had gone out of all of us as well. Do you remember?"

"Yes, Angelo, I remember how it was. Is it gone? Is it all gone?"

"I hope not, Juniper. You and I and the others, through Francis, we were privileged to touch, for a moment of time, another realm, another way of life where God shone in the darkness, the Kingdom of God. I remember those moments, the way it was. But there are others, there will be others in future times, who will not have known Francis, will not have the memories that we do. I want to let them know how it was. I want to tell them what it was like to have known Francis of Assisi."